I0636794

Boundaries Without

The Calumet Editions
2017 Anthology of Speculative Fiction

Edited by
Cynthia Kraack
and
Steve McEllistrem

CALUMET
EDITIONS
Minneapolis

CALUMET EDITIONS

Minneapolis

SECOND EDITION DECEMBER 2022
BOUNDARIES WITHOUT. The Calumet Editions 2017 Anthology of
Speculative Fiction. Copyright © 2016 by Calumet Editions.
All rights reserved.

"Unpleasantness at 20,000 Feet" by Terry Faust originally appeared in *Tinted Waters* edited by Michael Merriam. (Sam's Dot Publishing) 2012.

"Shift" by Nancy Holder originally appeared in *Doom City* edited by Charles L. Grant. (Tom Doherty Assoc LLC) 1987.

"Everything in Its Place" by Lyda Morehouse appeared in *Tales of the Unanticipated* (#19), August 1998.

"Divination by Water" by Pedro Ponce appeared in *PALABRA Literary Magazine*, Issue 4, 2008.

10 9 8 7 6 5 4 3 2

ISBN: 978-1-960250-02-5

Cover and book design: Gary Lindberg

Boundaries Without

The Calumet Editions
2017 Anthology of Speculative Fiction

Edited by

Cynthia Kraack
and
Steve McEllistrem

Contents

Introduction

Speculative fiction has always held a special place in our hearts. It challenges us to see the world in different ways, to imagine the possibilities of a darker or perhaps just different future than the one we might imagine ourselves, of an alternate present, of a past that might have led us to a different reality than the one we currently experience.

At its best, it draws us into a universe we long to explore from the safety and comfort of our armchairs. It can send chills down our spine or leave us laughing at the absurdity of a bizarre situation.

But it also compels us to examine our beliefs, not just in the way the world works, but also in how we sense that world. Is there something in the environment that could radically alter how we live? Are ghosts real? Do aliens exist? Will technology lead us to our doom? Perhaps it will save us from our darker impulses.

All these questions can be addressed and answered by speculative fiction, and every answer returns us to two related questions: is that possible and what if it is?

The laws of physics seem immutable, yet in these stories they sometimes bend and twist in devious ways. Perhaps we are nothing more than holograms in some greater cosmic entertainment. If so, is it possible for us to know that or to change it in any way?

We cannot be certain that our reality is the only reality, that our universe is the only universe. We cannot be certain that our minds are not playing tricks on us. We make assumptions about the world because we have to in order to get through the day, but what if we're wrong?

What if the world we think is real in fact contains creatures we hadn't considered? What if the past is not as solid as we were led to believe? What if everything we know as truth is based on a lie?

This collection seeks to provide us with different worlds, different possibilities. Each author challenges us to think about our universe and our place in it. Together the stories ask us to consider that maybe, just maybe, those things that go bump in the night are outside our imagination. Or perhaps everything is part of our imagination and we are mere participants in a communal dream.

Whatever the truth, can we really know it? How secure is the foundation on which we build our principles, our tenets? If you desire only the reality you can see, hear, taste and feel, then perhaps this anthology is not for you. But if you believe, like we do, that there just might be something more out there, some circumstance or opportunity or creature we hadn't really considered before, then open your mind and let the alternatives enter.

Cynthia Kraack
Steve McEllistrem

Acknowledgements

The following selections in this anthology are reprinted, some in slightly different versions, by permission of the authors or their publishers:

"Unpleasantness at 20,000 Feet" by Terry Faust originally appeared in Tinted Waters edited by Michael Merriam. (Sam's Dot Publishing) 2012.

"Shift" by Nancy Holder originally appeared in Doom City edited by Charles L. Grant. (Tom Doherty Assoc LLC) 1987.

"Everything in Its Place" by Lyda Morehouse appeared in Tales of the Unanticipated (#19), August 1998.

"Divination by Water" by Pedro Ponce appeared in PALABRA Literary Magazine, Issue 4, 2008.

An Inconspicuous Ring

G. Bernhard Smith

No one mulling about in the Stanford Astrophysics Supercomputing Facility would guess that Nigel Edam has found the first true evidence of an advanced non-human civilization, but he has. He smiles a furtive smile and pecks at the computer keys. The staff hardly notices the gangly grad student hunched over the computer in the corner, his long brown hair gathered into a loose bun on top of his head. He's one of more than a dozen soon-to-be scientists in and out of the lab every day. But Nigel Edam is different. The new occultation methods he's developed have enabled him to forge an invisible bridge to another race of beings.

His palms are tacky with cold sweat. The more work Nigel does the more unsettled he becomes. The creepy thing about analyzing data from a new exo-planet is the feeling he's observing something dangerous, something outside his experience. Who are these other beings? What do they make of their own world? Do they know we're here, watching? Whatever life forms inhabit that distant planet have been whispering the secrets of their existence out to the universe for hundreds, maybe thousands or even millions of years, and Nigel's the only human being on Earth who can hear them.

He sighs, takes a bite of his apple and rubs at the two-day-old stubble on his chin. Everything about astrophysics today is strange. Here he sits in the antiseptic quiet of the lab, sending pointing instructions out to the James Webb space telescope and waiting for the return data to be beamed at light speed back to his PC. Something about this place makes him crave the darkness of a star-filled sky. Behind this workstation he's hardly connected to the world at all.

Nigel still hasn't told anyone of his discovery, which makes him feel like a high-tech voyeur, watching something unseemly he must keep to himself. When the first data from one of the stars in the Epsilon-Lyrae system implied not only an Earth-sized planet but an artificial orbital ring, he wanted to find Professor Baron and tell him everything. But then caution took hold, told him to calm down, to wait until he could verify the data. He didn't want to look like an ignoramus in front of his thesis professor. Word would spread that he was some kind of kook, or worse. Another two sessions and he had conclusive evidence that the ring orbiting the new planet was synthetic. Spectral analysis showed it was made of carbon compounds, likely a light carbon-fiber structure. Nothing like that forms naturally. Only an advanced civilization performs an engineering feat of that magnitude.

So now Nigel is sure. He leans back in his chair in the cool of the computer lab and grins, the feeling of fullness in his belly crowding out the worry. He should tell Professor Baron about the data, but he can't. After two days' work validating his conclusions something sumptuous has crept into the equation—the knowing. Knowing something no one else in the world knows—it has become juicy, like the taste of a meaty porterhouse steak melting in his mouth. Seven billion people on Earth, and not one of them knows what he knows: that we are not alone. It tastes bloody and rare, rich, fulfilling in a scandalous way. They're out there. Not some pie-in-the-sky prospect, not some film director's idea of creepy movie aliens or even E.T., but another intelligent species. Mysterious beings, they exist, and Nigel's the only man on Earth who can prove it.

* * *

"You see that PBS thing on particle physicists a few years back? I think it was a NOVA," Professor Baron asks him as they walk together. Baron's left his car parked all the way out at the stadium lot so that his teen-aged daughter can come by and practice her driving. The early evening air is moist, a hint of salt in the breeze, each wave of wind bringing with it a feeling of connection, the ocean toying with Nigel's senses.

"Pardon?" Nigel says, sniffing the air.

"You don't watch TV?"

"I haven't lately, no. A NOVA you say?"

"It's an old episode. John Westin's in it."

Westin is the latest Stanford stand-out physicist, a thirty-something genius who believes he's isolated a new sub-atomic particle. His field of study is a branch of physics hardly related to Nigel's. Westin's one of those California wunderkinds with long blond hair and sandals who's become more phenomenon than scientist. Nigel's never met him, but he's met enough fair-haired West Coast genius scholars to know that he already hates the guy.

"I swear, particle physicists are more philosophers than scientists," says Baron chuckling.

"The field's played itself out," says Nigel. "As soon as CERN ramps up to double power they'll fill in all the missing standard model particles and then what? Guys like him'll be stuck teaching boring principles to bored undergraduates."

"Well, don't tell that to Westin on Saturday."

"What?"

"His party. You're not going to John Westin's birthday party?"

"I wasn't invited."

"Well, shit. I'm inviting you. You need to be there. The entire department's going. Chemistry department too. It's at his mother's place. Some mansion north of San Mateo. I'll send you directions." Professor Baron brushes back wisps of his thinning black hair. Nigel can't imagine why the man doesn't just shave it down short. In this wind he looks as if hundreds of black antennae have sprung from his head.

"What's the big deal with this man's birthday party?" Nigel asks.

"Everyone wants to bask in the glow of fame," Baron tells him, and then laughs. "I shouldn't say that. John's a great guy. You ought to meet him."

"Are you sure?" Professor Baron never stops trying to make Nigel feel welcome here at Stanford. No matter, Nigel's terrible at parties. He's attended three since arriving here from Wyoming and not one of them has had the desired effect.

"You have to. I've been telling Westin all about your work. Besides, it'll be fun. They'll be loads of young women there just dying to meet the would-be legend."

"So?"

"So, he's engaged."

"I don't follow."

Baron clears his throat. "That means that the girls will all be disappointed and will likely be… uh, amenable to other advances. Really, Nigel, you need to get out more."

Nigel tries to keep up with Baron's relentless walking pace. The man's just bought one of those fitness trackers. He's become obsessed with making his daily step goal.

"So," Baron says, "what's the latest on the Lyra system scan? You run across anything interesting?"

A feeling comes over Nigel, like air pumping into the empty chasm of his stomach. But then his shoulders straighten, and the electricity of knowing his secret prevails over the gurgle in his belly. He can tell Baron next week. The world won't come to an end. "Nothing yet."

"That Epsilon double-double has always been interesting to me, ever since I was a little kid. And now to know you've run across the possibility of planets in the goldilocks zones of two of the stars. I can't wait to see what you find." Baron turns and heads out toward a mercury-vapor lamp shining at the far corner of the stadium parking lot. Nigel peels away west, headed toward his flat. After a few moments Baron turns and calls back, "See you on Saturday."

Nigel waves.

* * *

"Occlusion technology," he tells her.

"What the hell is that?" Beth Greener asks him. Nigel knows it must be boring but he can't stop himself. They're alone, sitting together on a wide white sofa in the Westin family living room, a space larger than his entire apartment. The ocean air wafting in from the balcony smells of salt spray and rocky surf. On the wall behind them an original Jackson Pollack painting looms, hanging there like a gray-black curtain splashed with fiery daubs of yellow and orange. Before them the last rays of evening pour through a floor-to-ceiling window, its massive glass panes cantilevered out from bottom to top, offering a god-like view of the bay below. This woman's eyes share the same hue as the darkening ocean. Nigel can only glance into them for a moment before his self-consciousness forces him to look away and down to the near incalculable expanse of water. He wonders about the depths of the bay, and the ocean beyond, and the world behind this woman's blue eyes.

What is she thinking? Is she interested in him, or his work, or neither? Is she being polite? Perhaps she's the rare bird who'd be fascinated. She smells lovely, like the marigolds his sister used to grow in the garden outside their parents' front door. He answers her question, even though he assumes those deep indigo irises will soon roll to the back of her head.

"Now that we can resolve light from distant star systems with the Webb Space Telescope," he tells her, clasping his hands together so he doesn't start waving them around like a madman, "we need some way to block the glare from the bright central star, or any light source really, so that we can see what else is there."

"What else could be there?"

His hands leap out and spread upward like a minister's at Sunday services. "Everything!" Tresses of his hair scatter in all directions. "Planets, asteroids, comets—anything you can think of, other civilizations perhaps!"

The woman has held it together for a few minutes, nodding her head and trying not to giggle, but now she bursts out laughing. "You're passionate about this, I see."

Nigel lowers his arms and stares at her. "This is serious," he tells her, quieter than the moment before. Nigel wants more than life itself to impress women, but he's become sure that a life filled with female conquests is not in his future. The first person he saw tonight was Beth Greener. She answered the door, a small young woman, blond with clear-framed glasses, a toothy white smile and the hands of a goddess.

He thrust out his own hand at her. He couldn't help himself. His mother had taught him to always extend his hand in friendship when meeting someone new. It had become a habit, reflex. The kids in his elementary school laughed at him when he did it, but whether he had some undiagnosed mental condition or just incurably good manners, Nigel couldn't break from floating his stupid lily-white palm out toward anyone to whom he'd been introduced. A moment after she opened the door out popped his hand, him standing there like some awkward schoolboy. She laughed at him, but like most people would, she extended her hand in return, introduced herself. For so small a person she had magnificently long fingers, and long nails painted a dark shade of red.

When she took back her palm, he hoped the crooked lower teeth in his smile hadn't gotten in the way of things, hadn't somehow negated the charge he thought he'd detected in her eyes. After an introduction to some of her friends in the Chemistry Department she led him over to a long white sofa, sat him down and asked him what he was working on. And now she is laughing at his answer. He surmises that her fascination with him, or his work, or perhaps her patience with his demeanor has worn thin.

"You probably wouldn't understand the importance of what I do," he tells her, and turns away. Nigel has begun letting the sting of these rejections show on the outside, although he can't figure out why. His ears burn with embarrassment. He never used to let on that people hurt him, but why take it out on her? He considers getting up and launching himself toward the kitchen to check for refreshments.

"You're right," she tells him, just as he's made up his mind to extricate himself from her attention. She reaches out and grabs one of his wrists. "I bet hardly anyone does, or would, understand the importance of your work, I mean. But aren't we all like that?"

He catches a glimpse of her eyes. "Aren't we all like what?"

"I mean, almost everyone here is an intellectual egg-head doing ground-breaking research of one sort or another, but don't we all feel misunderstood? Like who we are and what we're all about is so important, only other people don't seem to realize it?"

Her fingers gripping his wrist are almost an apology. "Sure. I guess you're right." Nigel smiles. "What is it you do, if I might ask?"

She smiles at him, takes back her hand. "I teach Chemistry to undergrads. I'm an adjunct. I was a bright star before I got my Ph.D. at Washington, and then I moved here and fell into complete obscurity, just one of the myriad of twinkling lights in a department full of mega-minds. I was lucky to land a position at all." ‘

"But you must have had something fascinate you into further study."

"Carbon-filament bonding—I'm an organic chemist."

Nigel can almost feel the click. The ring around his little world, the one that proves the intelligence of something out there in the deep darkness of space—the means to understand that ring is this woman's expertise. She is no longer some unfathomable mystery to Nigel. She has become a resource, a gateway to something big and new.

"So," she continues, suddenly amused. "I can see your eyes glazing over."

"No. Hardly."

"And yet you believe that who you are is so much more important than who the rest of us think we are."

"I don't mean me, or what I think I am," Nigel tells her, the shyness about his strong feelings melting. "I'm talking only about what I do."

"But isn't that who you are, really? I mean, most guys think of themselves as the sum total of what they do."

It's like she's seen through some bright light and managed to stare right into the dark well of him. "I guess you're right. But, I mean, what I'm doing is really important."

"So why is what you're doing so much more important than what the rest of us are doing?" She stares, her dark eyes boring holes into him.

"I've discovered something. Something that no one else on Earth knows about."

"What?" Now she's sitting on the edge of her seat, her eyes sparkling.

"I… I can't say…"

The lights dim and a beautiful older woman with short blond hair walks into the dining area at the far end of the living room carrying a lighted birthday cake for John Westin. A couple dozen people standing near the dining table turn toward her and those following behind start clapping.

"That's John's mother," Beth tells Nigel, her attention suddenly shifting to the grand entrance.

"You know her?" Nigel asks.

Beth laughs. "I ought to. She's going to be my mother-in-law in a few months."

Nigel's heart sinks, like some World War II U-boat crushed by a depth charge, hammered by an invisible explosion deep down, in a place no one else can see.

"I didn't know you were engaged," Nigel says, his tone low and quiet. He looks down at her beautiful hands, her lithe fingers. "I don't see any ring."

"I don't know why I didn't tell you before. I'm sorry. John's not big on tradition. His mother's even worse. She wonders why anyone today even entertains the notion of marriage."

Nigel stares at the woman with the cake. "She doesn't look too steady on her feet."

"She's plastered. She's been drinking since three this afternoon. It's a wonder she can walk at all." Nigel looks back at Beth in time to catch a guarded frown.

Party guests begin singing, "Happy Birthday," each of them searching for the correct starting note. The woman, weaving into the room, cake in hand, takes two steps, trips on the carpeting and falls forward into a knot of onlookers, tossing the cake against the rather substantial chest of a gorgeous young thing who in turn pitches her drink over her shoulder, drenching the man behind her in margarita. Everyone bursts into laughter, Westin's mother recovering nicely and then struggling to help pick up the cake. The girl who was the cake's target is not so fortunate. Icing all over the front of her blouse, the girl shrieks and then falls to her knees crying. The birthday song dwindles and then dies.

Beth springs from the conversation with Nigel, rushes over and, bending down, helps the girl to her feet. She escorts the cake victim to the bathroom while the rest of the drunken cackling horde make merry at her expense, their alcohol-saturated sensibilities unaffected by the girl's predicament. But Nigel has not been unaffected; he is now in love with Beth Greener.

Love: was it a realization one came upon, a conclusion, or was it something outside the self, something like a blanket of stars thrown over your head? Nigel traces his feelings, his astonishment at Beth's empathy for the girl with the cake all over her. He can't shake the whole of Beth from his mind—her smile, her fingers, her willingness to listen, her seeing him, understanding his character in an instant, her figure, which he'd only gotten to appreciate after she'd dashed away to help—all of it the image of a woman Nigel hardly knows, variables in a mysterious equation that seem to equal love. Are the mysterious quantities real, or are they all imaginary, the product of a hormone-manufactured delusion? Strange.

Nigel was in love once before, in high school, and that was the unrequited sort, the sort that turned into an embarrassing fiasco where he declared his feelings for his classmate after French class one afternoon and she told him to fuck off or she'd tell the instructor he was harassing her, which in truth he had been, but it had only been going on for a week or two. Would his whole life be full of women telling him to get lost, the entire gender-group a secret alien civilization an unspannable distance away?

Nigel always wanted to study at a big-name prestigious university, but now he wishes he had never come. He sits on this isolated couch in a dark corner and wonders whether being here, whether doing his Ph.D. work at Stanford is as bad a decision as having extended his palm to Beth Greener. He wishes the testosterone in him were something else, alcohol or perhaps adrenaline. Being infatuated is messy and diversionary. At this moment millions or perhaps billions of individuals, members of an alien race light-years from Earth, are hard at work doing whatever it is they're doing, while Nigel sits at a party pining for another man's fiancée.

He bursts out laughing. It's funny, really, hilarious. He laughs so loud people gathered around in the dining room stop paying attention to the now-defunct cake spread all over the floor and start staring at Nigel. Some point at him, and then a few of them start laughing too.

Nigel rises to his feet and rushes down a dark hallway toward the john where Beth and the cake victim have taken shelter. The sound of low moaning sobs drifts out in fits and stops from under the lavatory door. He knocks.

"Uh... Beth?"

"Yeah?"

"It's Nigel."

"Yeah?"

"Could you come out here, please?"

The door to the bathroom cracks open. Beth's face emerges, her shoulder leaning against the door's edge. Nigel rubs at the back of his neck as she stares up at him.

"You going to be much longer?" he asks her.

"We're trying to get cleaned up. What do you want?"

"Um, I don't know. I thought I'd go, but I didn't want to leave without talking to you." Nigel's stomach is turning fits inside his abdomen. What on earth is he doing?

Beth looks at him and smirks. "You want to talk?"

"I mean, I wanted to know if you could see me."

She busts out laughing, but then catches herself. After quieting down she puts her hand over her mouth. "You're serious." She lowers her voice. "I'm seeing someone else, Nigel. I'm engaged."

"I don't care."

Beth laughs up at him.

Nigel bends to her, his lips searching down, but instead of seeking her lips he curls to the side and kisses her cheek, lingers there a moment, his cheekbone nestled up against her glasses. He rises back to full height and stares down at her again. She's not laughing anymore. For a moment her eyes are closed, but when she opens them again she frowns. "I hardly know you."

"Yes. Well, I don't do this well." Nigel's head droops. Someone from the party enters the hallway and sees them. He stares for a few seconds, his eyebrows rise, and then he turns and heads back toward the living room.

"I need to talk to someone," Nigel manages to whisper.

She stares into his eyes. He can't tell whether she understands his need for her or not. She begins to speak. "I…"

"Don't say no."

She takes a step out of the doorway and pauses. She's standing next to him, resting her open palms against his chest. The smell of her flowery perfume drifts past his nose. "I'm spoken for." She looks down at her feet, then back up into his eyes. "Please."

"Right." Nigel turns and storms back toward the living room. He stops at the entrance to the hallway and finally spots John Westin talking to a knot of worshipers huddled around him near the entrance to the kitchen. Nigel hurries toward Westin, sifting his way around other party-goers who are oblivious to the notion that aliens exist, that they could be watching us, might arrive here at any moment. He shoves his way between two young women holding drinks, the sound of the ice tinkling brightly through the banter. A moment later he's standing face to face with the star. He stops, pushes out his hand toward Westin.

"I'm Nigel Edam," he tells him, smoothing a strand of his hair back over his ear with his other hand.

Westin smiles. "I know, I know! Professor Baron's been raving about your work at faculty meetings." Westin reaches out and grabs Nigel's hand, shaking it up and down. "Ultra-high resolution digital occlusion filters! It sounds amazing."

Nigel feels a rush. He can't help being attracted to Westin's smile, his big white California teeth reflecting off the black of his turtleneck. He's not as tall as Nigel, but he has something intangible Nigel envies: he's likeable. It's maddening. The whole academic and scientific environment makes it nearly impossible to be human. But this guy is good looking, cordial, and impressive in a self-deprecating yet accessible way. The whole aura the guy gives off is frustrating. It doesn't matter. Nigel doesn't want to be this man's friend; he wants the woman.

"What about Beth?" he asks Westin.

"Beth? What about Beth?" The space between Westin's eyebrows crumples into a single wrinkle.

"She doesn't..."

Nigel can't finish the sentence because he doesn't know what to say. She doesn't love him, doesn't want him, doesn't understand him the way she understands Nigel? What is it about what she's said to Nigel that in ten minutes has penetrated into his psyche? What is it about her that has occulted his sense of reason? Her glasses? Her long fingers? The red polish on her nails?

"She doesn't what?" Westin asks him now, his jaws snapping back closed and tightening as he stares into Nigel's eyes.

"She doesn't..." Nigel struggles to end his sentence. He wants to say, "love you!" or "need you!" or something even more devastating, like "know that you even exist!" but instead he shrugs. "...know how lucky she is."

The muscles in Westin's neck loosen, and then he smiles like a cat. "C'mon, we should get you a drink," he tells Nigel, grabbing his elbow and leading him toward the counter with the booze. By the time only ice remains in his glass he doesn't know whether being infatuated with Beth Greener is crazier than believing in aliens.

* * *

The undergrads file out one by one, each on their way to another classroom. Most look as if they've been bombarded by a futuristic light ray that's pasted a blank stare upon their faces. Some grumble about multivalent bonding and tetrahedral structured carbon molecules. When the stream of students thins Nigel squeezes through the door and paces up to the lecture podium where Beth Greener stands, staring down at her notes. She looks up.

"Nigel?"

"I'm glad you remembered me," he says, unable to meet her gaze. He reaches up and hands her a graph paper printout upon which is depicted a squiggly line with bumps, peaks and troughs.

She takes the sheet from him. "What's this?"

"I'm hoping you can tell me."

She glances at the page again. "Looks like a spectral analysis readout."

"Yes, that's exactly what it is. I was hoping you could identify the composition of the element or elements." Nigel smiles and looks into her eyes, the blue of them lighter here with the midday sun beaming in.

She smiles back and then takes a more fervent look at the graph. "Whatever it is it contains a lot of carbon. There's an oxygen peak—two oxygen peaks, nitrogen and several heavier elements. Is this the light spectrum from a star?" Before he can answer she adds, "It can't be a star, there's hardly any hydrogen or helium."

"You're right. It's not a star." Nigel is amazed at Beth's supposition. She's already leaping to the correct conclusions.

"But it's a celestial object?"

"Yes."

"Naturally formed?"

"Why do you ask?"

"These spikes between the oxygen peaks would imply this is a complex compound, some sort of carbon polymer. This can't have formed in nature. It's got to be man-made."

Nigel chuckles. "It's not man-made, I assure you."

Beth's eyebrows curl down and the bridge of her nose tightens. She smirks. "Impossible. This is artificial. Nothing like this forms in nature." Having drawn her conclusion she looks up into his eyes and smiles. "That's probably not what you want to hear, is it?"

Nigel's heart is leaping up and down. An organic chemist has confirmed his conclusion without the slightest clue of what she has done.

"What if I told you to consider alternatives?" he asks her. "What are the possibilities?"

Beth laughs, that same hearty laugh she laughed three days ago at John Westin's party. Nigel is beginning to enjoy the sound of that laugh. She looks down at the page again and begins thinking aloud. They're now alone in the classroom.

"Hmm. OK. So, you say this is indeed a celestial object, but that it is not man-made. It's a carbon structure that cannot form in nature, and it is not a star. I'm not aware of anything that fits these parameters." Her eyes reach back up to his. Something like wonder is swimming around inside them. "Is this some kind of joke?"

"No, I assure you this is very real." Nigel searches for some way to draw Beth toward a conclusion. "What if I told you I observed this structure in orbit around a distant earth-like planet? One circling a star about 162 light years away."

"I would say that would mean..." Beth's hand rises slowly to her mouth. She looks down at the paper and then back up into Nigel's eyes. "Oh my God!" she says, almost whispering. Then louder, "This is not... I mean, you must be... Nigel, is this real?"

Nigel smiles, his heart beating like a cannon going off inside his chest. "It is. It's a ring, an artificial ring, around a tiny planet in Epsilon Lyrae. I didn't lie, the ring's not man-made." He laughs. "Hell, I don't know who made it, but they aren't human. I wanted you to be the first person I show it to. You can even be an independent source of confirmation that I cite in my thesis," he says, chuckling. "Good thing you're an organic chemist."

Sharing this moment with Beth is so much more rewarding than telling Baron. Sure, Professor Baron would hoot and want to break open champagne bottles, but telling this to Beth is so much more important. He feels a connection to something new telling Beth about this. She will wonder about what the ring is, about what it means. She'll have a personal and professional interest in something he has given her, and he's the only man in the world who could have done that.

Beth smiles, and then shrieks, the scream echoing through the empty classroom and down the now-deserted hallway. She runs around her podium and grabs Nigel by the neck, throwing her weight against him, taking mini-jumps and tugging him around in circles. "Nigel! Aren't you happy about this?"

Nigel is happy, but the screaming has set his nerves on edge. "Shh! No one else knows about this. No one else in the entire world. Do you know what a panic it could create?" Beth stops jumping around and holds him out at arm's length. Her eyebrows rise and tighten to her forehead, a puckish smile on her face. She closes her mouth and then pretends to button it closed with her fingers.

"I can't believe this," she says, and then she reaches up and kisses Nigel on the mouth.

It happens so fast Nigel is not prepared for it. Beth pulls away, and then a strange realization seems to come over her. She shrugs and then grimaces like she's kissed him by accident. Nigel bends and kisses her flush on the lips, lingers there, pulling her body close to his. When he releases her, her eyes are closed, the way they were at the party on Saturday when he kissed her cheek.

"Before," Nigel says, his voice breathy, his head swimming with stars, "you said you never got a ring, but I'm giving this one to you. And until we tell someone, it's our secret, something no one else in this world knows about."

Impulse Control

CM Kerley

The silver sedan slowed to a stop on the slippery street, parking under the anemic glow of the stuttering streetlamp outside number 96. A steady snowfall had started a few hours earlier. Steve cut the rumbling engine, the sudden silence instantly filled by the sizzle of snowflakes landing on the steaming hood. He opened the door and stepped out into ankle-deep drifts. As he walked up the path to the house, he smiled; the crunch of the snow under his leather winter boots reminded him of biting into the fresh hot garlic bread he'd had with his dinner earlier that night. He stopped.

Looking up, he saw his colleague Ben's flabby silhouette in the living room window.

"Asshole," he muttered. From the way the shadow was shaking he was either laughing or choking. Steve gave the silhouette the finger, stomped back to the car and took the bag of leftovers from the back seat. Steve retraced his steps up the path to the house, unconsciously stepping into the tracks he'd left a minute before. The house was like all the others on the street—single story red bricks, a wide porch running the length of the front with wind chimes hanging outside the front door. As he put his key in the door and turned the lock he noticed someone had changed the house numbers to 69.

"Again!" he yelled into the dark still night. He turned his key and went in, slamming the door closed. He took off his thick winter coat, gloves and scarf, and leaned down to touch the radiator; he knew it was on, but touching it made him believe it. He checked his pockets without paying attention to why, and then gestured at the man waiting for him in the lounge.

"Come on," Ben said, walking over to him, taking the bag of leftovers, opening it and breathing in the rich aromas of herbs and tomato sauce, "night shift started two minutes ago, we're late."

"Because of your little joke back there." Steve half-heartedly accused.

"Me?" Ben feigned indignation as they headed for the basement. "Prove it."

* * *

"Did you see the memo from head office this morning?" Ben asked between mouthfuls of reheated lasagne. He was sitting at the small table in the back of the room, away from the wall covered floor-to-ceiling in screens and the desk littered with keyboards connected to hard drives stacked atop each other. Steve didn't reply straight away, instead he nodded vigorously and held up his hand. Ben waited a minute until his friend was done reading the code that cascaded across the screens.

"They're releasing the phase-seven prototype into the water system next week," Steve said by way of acknowledging the question. He clicked off the code screen and initiated all the live feeds from the hidden cameras in all the houses on the block. Each screen came to life with different images from the rooms inside the houses.

"I checked the original timetables. The sevens are about a month ahead of schedule." Steve's usually cynical tone brightened up. "At this rate, if the tests of this round are as good as the last one, we could be getting our phase bonus before Christmas instead of after."

"That'd be great." Ben savored the last mouthful, chewing a little slower and moving the fork around the empty foil container, as if bumping around the sides would make another forkful magically appear. "Michelle wants to get away for the holidays, visit her parents in Florida for about a week, but the credit card is maxed. She keeps bringing it up, starting to annoy me."

"Is her dad the one with the fishing boat hire company?"

"No, that's her brother Pete. Her dad has, had," he corrected himself with a click of the tongue, "the realtor agencies that he sold before the bubble burst. She's mentioned it a few hundred times this year already."

Steve winced in sympathy.

"I know what you mean. I've got a list of things in the house that need replacing. Every time the kids come home from college they need a ton of new stuff. A bit of extra cash helps with the chaos."

Ben shrugged, licked his already cleaned fork one more time, then changed the subject.

"There's a bunch of fliers that came with the mail yesterday, voting crap for the new wanna-be mayor." Ben reached into the bag of leftovers to see what else Steve had brought him, knowing there'd be an array of desserts.

"Do we have to vote?" Steve asked.

"Head office wants Beckett in the seat and we've got to fix the neighborhood." Ben pointed at a piece of paper covered in coffee stains. "Code is there for voting day; I've already put it into my phone. Any ideas of speeding up deployment? I don't want to miss Big Brother. It's eviction night." He picked out a pastry and stuffed it into his mouth, waiting for Steve's answer.

"Carpool everyone to the polling station, jack the phone into the car stereo and deploy the music, whatever's the latest number one on the stations."

Ben nodded, chewing loudly. He sighed happily as he devoured the treat from the bag. Steve looked at the lines of numbers and symbols on the page, reading it like a recipe, ignoring the coffee stains and sticky edges.

"Very neat," was his only comment. He switched one of the screens back to the code, leaned over to a keyboard across the desk, punched in some numbers and looked over at the image pulled to the center screen.

"Hey, Ben, what's this?" He turned and stared expectantly.

"What's what?" His tone was innocent but his wicked grin gave it away. The silence lasted almost a minute. "I wasn't sure you'd spot it." Ben kicked his feet against the floor and his old office chair rolled over to the desk, slotting him neatly beside Steve.

"Okay." He clapped his hands together to start his confession. "So, it's Wednesday, nothing ever happens here on a Wednesday, you know that," his grin got wider, "and we're testing muscular management, right?"

"We're testing impulse management," Steve corrected.

"Potato po-tah-toe." Ben shrugged, ignoring the incredulous look from his friend. "I hate Wednesdays." He started to twirl on his chair. "The husbands go to work. The wives go shopping or visit each other and talk about nothing. The kids go to school, come home, stare at the TV. It's boring."

"Can't disagree with you there," Steve pulled a cigarette from the packet crumpled inside his coat pocket, put it to his dry lips, lit it and took a long slow pull, savoring the first burn of hot smoke.

"I thought you quit?"

Steve shook his head as he took another drag.

"Still trying," the words came out as smoke, "kind of ironic, hey?"

Ben laughed and spun on his chair again.

"Anyway," Steve waved from Ben to the screen, the cigarette slowly burning between his fingers, "you were about to tell me why there's test code in today's logs when we didn't have anything scheduled."

"Well, when you put it like that." Ben stopped spinning, pulled himself up to the desk and started tapping on the keyboard, the image on the screen fast-forwarding. "Number 43, the one with the short hair, my favorite tester?"

"Likes coffee with sugar, constantly washing her hands, reads a lot of crime drama."

"That's her." Ben pointed at the screen. "Watch this." He slowed it down to normal speed and hit play.

On the screen, a woman with short hair sat on a couch in a living room watching TV with a cup of coffee.

"Watch closely or you'll miss it."

Steve leaned forward, closer to the screen.

The woman twitched and shifted in her seat.

"There!" Ben shouted triumphantly. "I entered the code and her reaction was almost instantaneous."

"These phase sixes are good," Steve agreed and took another drag on the cigarette, pulling deeply, eyes never leaving the screen. "The latency after command is down to only a couple of minutes. What did you send?" He stubbed out the cigarette.

"I made her hungry and I sent a sub-command too, you'll see, just watch."

"Hungry?" Steve cocked his head, reaching for another cigarette. "We did the basics already. Why you wasting time on that?"

Ben didn't answer, he just pointed at the screen.

"Five," he said.

The woman shifted in her seat again and looked around the room.

"Four."

She scratched her elbow and moved to stand.

"Three." Ben started to chuckle. "Keep watching."

Steve leaned closer still.

"Two."

The woman got up and walked across the living room toward the kitchen.

"One."

She tripped over her own feet and fell forward with a shriek. Ben and Steve burst out laughing.

The woman took a second before picking herself up off the floor and rubbing a sore knee. She turned around, looked at the floor as if expecting to see something there to explain why she had just tripped.

The two men laughed until she walked off the screen. Steve leaned back, reached over, and clapped his hands in front of Ben's face.

"Oh, shit," he choked between laughing and taking a drag, "her face!"

"I know, I must have watched it twenty times already." Ben rolled to the desk and pulled the keyboard back toward himself, punching in more commands that sent images onto all the screens. Steve's eyes widened.

"Really?"

"Yup," Ben deadpanned. "This phase six is a lot better than we thought, maybe even better than head office realizes. Especially if someone's just drunk something with water from the mains in it."

"Have you reported this?"

"Not yet, I was having too much fun. Watch these. I've had a busy afternoon."

* * *

The screens came to life, soundless images dubbed over by the laughter of the two men in the basement control room. On one screen a weary middle-aged man yawned at his reflection in the mirror. He rubbed at the day's stubble on his chin and tipped his head back, flaring his nostrils. The man looked down at the bottles and tubes set out neatly on the bathroom cabinet over the sink. The man reached for the tube of toothpaste.

Ben grabbed Steve's shoulder, shuddering from laughter.

The man put his hand on the toothpaste, stopped, his hand twitching slightly.

Ben put his fist into his mouth and squeezed his eyes shut to try to stop the tears of laughter.

The man looked at the toothpaste, but instead of picking it up his hand moved over to another tube. He picked it up and squeezed it onto his toothbrush.

Sweat beaded along Ben's brow.

The man turned on the tap and took a mouthful of water before putting his toothbrush to his mouth. A second later, as if he had just been punched in the face, the man gagged and yanked the toothbrush out, wild eyes in shock. He bent over and started to spit. Fumbling for the tap, he turned it on, desperately slurping water into his mouth to clean it out.

Steve wheezed between sucks on his cigarette.

The man cleaned out his mouth. They could see him shouting and a moment later his wife rushed in looking confused and alarmed. The man was talking quickly, trying to explain why he was holding a tube of hemorrhoid cream in his hand instead of toothpaste.

After an hour the two men calmed down. Steve opened a new pack of cigarettes. Ben finished the last donut, licking the sugar off his fingers.

"Seriously though, these results are impressive. Have you spoken to any of the other guys in the neighborhood on the other blocks, or in the city?"

"I sent a few messages out. A couple guys a few blocks over are going to try a few things tonight and see what happens. Michael over in Cresswell Heights said there's a party across from him tonight. A bunch of neighbors are getting together for their Bible study. He's pretty sure one of the husbands is gay so I sent him a script."

"For what?"

"Hand movements mainly, basic touching," Ben said, sitting back, satisfied with himself.

"That's a bit far, isn't it, what if he's not gay?" Steve rubbed his forehead with a nicotine-stained yellow finger.

Ben stared at him.

"Who cares? It's a harmless hand on the leg or whatever Michael does with it."

Steve chuckled. "I can just imagine it." He feigned a look of complete shock and changed his voice, pretending to lurch at Ben. "Jesus, sorry, man. I don't know what came over me, I'm not gay, I swear, it must've been the wine, I tripped or something."

They started to laugh again.

"Yeah." Ben nodded, mimicking Steve's voice. "The devil made me do it." He got up and went to the small fridge near the far wall, taking out a cold Coke. Cracking open the can, he took a long drink.

"Head office is going to flip when they get wind of this." Ben wiped the sweet chemical drink from his lips, enjoying the tingle from the carbonation. "These bio-bots are much easier to program than anything we've seen before." He pulled up another screen of code. "Look at this though." Ben handed him sheets printed hours ago, already crumpled and dog-eared.

Steve lit another cigarette and started to read.

"Memory loss?"

"Only for a second. If the code trips out, it feels like déjà vu apparently, so nothing to worry about, quick little electric shock and then they reset."

"The next phase of upgrades going to fix that?"

Ben shrugged.

"How should I know?" he said in his best *Star Trek* voice. "I'm a programmer, damnit, not a brain doctor." The two chuckled and lapsed into silence.

"Seriously though," Ben said, unusually somber as he watched the screens. "Can you imagine how far this could go?"

Steve tapped his forehead.

"We're only at phase six and we're seeing these results. By phase ten, who knows?"

"It's getting easier to deploy as well; we could move out of this crappy basement if they get the signal spread right."

The two men sat lost in their thoughts, imagining giving the news to head office and what the reaction would be.

"This would definitely get us promoted."

The two men settled back into their chairs and turned back to watching the screens, flicking through the houses on the block, observing as everyone slept. On one screen, a woman with short hair grimaced in her sleep, rolled over, a headache keeping her from slipping into deep sleep. The covers fell away from her as she moved, but in the dark of her room the secret cameras couldn't pick out the bruise on her knee. She dreamed she was driving a car down a steep cliff road. There were rocks and the car was out of control, crashing into the rocks, going faster and faster until eventually it careened off the cliff edge. She jerked awake, muscles twitching, throat dry.

"Babe?" her husband murmured. "Headaches again?"

"It's nothing." She rubbed her head. "Just a bad dream. I can't even remember it already."

"Get some water, take a headache tablet, you'll feel better."

Refugee in Paris

Cynthia. Kraack

Monday night. Wind steals the weak warmth of a November day. Jeffrey and I gather among other Americans caught in Paris. We stay close to each other as rain begins. Jeffrey urges me to move closer to the church doors.

People brush against each other, push for position. Jeffrey slides inches to the left and tilts a shoulder to keep an older man from cutting in front of us. I follow my husband's directions, turn to face the church's massive wooden doors. Wind slaps my cheek. People crush so close I'm not able to lift a hand to raise my scarf.

We wear good rubberized European boots with liners to hold warmth. In the jostling crowd, I don't worry about slipping on the damp stones underfoot. Jeffrey found the boots in an abandoned automobile, and after that I knew we had a fighting chance to survive the streets.

It is my fault we stayed that extra day in Paris. I scheduled a client meeting the day after Jeffrey's presentation. It is my fault we arrived at the airport as news began flooding the world that after three weeks of fighting a killing influenza, North America had closed its borders. It is my fault we live on the streets after French hotels expelled Americans for fear of infection.

The official story circulates that the government can't help the many tourists caught in the crisis because they must deal with hundreds of thousands of poor Parisians who hope to survive the winter. Mornings we see bodies piled at the mouths of metro stops, stripped of clothing. Perhaps the government is telling the truth. Without clothes, no one knows a dead person's country of origin. The virus carrier could have been a tourist from Cleveland or a banquier from the 16th arrondissement. Unmarked brown trucks collect corpses.

I hide food deep in a pouch under my coats. I clean for an old woman who occasionally pays me with food better than can be purchased in the foreigners' markets. Between Madame Lambert's food and finding odd jobs that keep us indoors during days, we stay healthy. Jeffrey's position as a physician-researcher allowed us to receive vaccinations before we left for six weeks in France, so we don't fear becoming infected.

"Now," Jeffrey says in my ear.

The pushing and shoving intensify. I slide my feet ahead of Jeffrey as he blocks potential interlopers. In five minutes we move inside the church and I race between the slower moving to the treasured circle where wood floors cover slate tiles and make sleeping more comfortable. Near the exact center of the church, I drop my coat to the floor and spread my body next to it. A hand lands near mine, feet touch the coat's edge. Jeffrey kicks aside an encroaching blanket.

"Good claim, Stephanie." Even through the sterile mask covering his nose and mouth, Jeffrey makes my name sound comforting. We will survive another day. American security guards will block the church's entrances and keep us safe from gangs that wander Paris. In limited light, we share our meal. Jeffrey leans in close to block the hungry stare of a skinny kid in multiple sweatshirts and no mask.

People around us feed their children, settle elderly relatives, and assess each other's health in the dimming light. Within the hour hundreds of flashlights will be the only break in the big church's inky darkness before the start of mandatory sleep hours.

"I have a big surprise." He pulls down his mask and leans

close. "I assisted Dr. Wagner today at the hospital. You remember sleeping in his attic?"

"He can take us back?" Wagner's attic was the last time we slept in a bed with sheets. We had survived on the streets for a week at that point. I hope Jeffrey will say yes or, even better, that he has found a way that we can go home to Chicago.

"No. He can't put his family at risk." Taking a bite of ham, he chews before talking. "He hired me to help with foreigners' care. Pay is decent. I'll get two meals a day and use of a locker and shower."

"That is good news." I lower my expectations and accept these developments as truly good, even if they don't take us closer to the end of exile.

"It gets better." Jeffrey leans closer to my ear. "I have a telephone extension."

I nearly stop breathing. We have not talked to anyone in the States since demand crashed the cell phone networks. "Did you call your father?"

"No, I called Northwestern University's emergency travel number. Told them where I could be reached."

I pull away.

"They told me the government's priority is to get essential professionals back in the States." Grabbing me, he holds me close as a parent might when calming a child. "The pandemic is horrific at home. It could be months before air travel is restored. We will be the first out."

"How are our families doing?" The damp church reminds me of a tomb. Will we survive as wandering sleepers? Money is useless with the French government banning Americans living among uninfected people. Squatting in empty buildings is too risky. We would not survive outdoor jail cells where foreigners are housed to avoid contaminating the French inmates.

"Maybe you can dig into the old lady's heart and convince her that a short time of defying the officials is a Christian action." Jeffrey draws me closer. "We have written documentation of our vaccinations."

Madame Lambert has promised me work consolidating the essentials from her two-floor apartment into one winter sleeping quarter in her salon.

Jeffrey burps, tainting the air between us. "Can you persuade her?"

I chew my bread and puzzle how to make our dangerous request sound safe for the old woman. "There's a butler's pantry off the kitchen. A mattress could be put in there."

"Fantastic."

"She's scared of being alone." Jeffrey moves away. I pack our food. "She has no one in Paris. One son is in Greenland, the other in Montreal."

We settle for the night on our sliver of floor. Cold threads through everything. "Grab the water bottle," Jeffrey whispers.

"I'll keep watch." I gather our belongings closer and watch as another frightening night unfolds within the nearly dark church.

A skinny arm circles my back. I bring up my elbow and make contact with a chin. There is a whimper and curses. The kid scrambles across a sleeping family to lift a bag and loaf of bread.

"Thief." I throw the word into the quiet. Watchers sit up in the midst of their groups. A man throws himself over the escaping child.

"Our bread. Our milk." A woman's voice rises. A baby cries.

"Get off me, you asshole." The boy is silenced as the sound of a fist connecting with flesh can be heard.

"Michael?" Somewhere a woman gives the thief a name. "Where are you?"

"He's staying with us the rest of the night," the boy's captor shouts.

Neither of us pays attention to the child's return to his mother in the morning. We empty out of the grand church-turned-refugee-warehouse into the cold.

"The virus has barely touched Paris. In the next few weeks foreigners will suffer even more," Jeffrey mutters. "Madam must give us a bed."

* * *

My employer is quiet. She didn't sleep well worrying about rumors of squatters invading homes. I put an arm around her shoulder. Her voice slips into a mess of French and English.

"What if my sons do not come?" She tries for calm. "I'm a reader, a talker, a shopper. None of these traits will keep me alive. My sons want me to find a live-in housekeeper."

Laws allow hiring foreigners but forbid providing shelter without proper permits. Some day I will return to my home and office in downtown Chicago, but today Madame Lambert's need for a housekeeper might keep us alive.

"Jeffrey and I have been vaccinated against this virus and he's been hired at the hospital. We could stay here and help you." My eyes focus on her. I want to hold her hands, keep her captive until I say everything I planned. She steps back. "I know there is a legal risk, but you would be physically safer."

She turns to gaze out a window. The smell of last night's dinner lingers in the salon, suggesting a hot meal of poultry and good coffee. Finally she breaks the silence. "You think you will not get sick, but Jeffrey might carry the virus into my home."

"Madame, let me be your assistant just while you look for a housekeeper." I speak to her as I would a client. "Jeffrey will stay upstairs."

She nods as if considering.

"We could put a mattress in the butler pantry for me." Not used to begging, my words halt.

"My dear." Moisture gathers in her eyes. "You are a middle-class American woman with a nice home of your own. How could you sleep in a pantry?" She wipes at tears with her left hand, thick diamond rings twinkling. "It is not appropriate."

"Not appropriate" barely describes the European Union's response to residents of countries where the pandemic began. I name the policy *xenophobic* and *inhumane*. Jeffrey says no country has the perfect response to this catastrophe. Everyone was caught flat-footed.

"If you spent evenings queuing in line to sleep on the floor of a church with hundreds of strangers, you'd understand that any mattress is attractive." My voice quivers.

Madame raises her head on a neck stiff with privilege. "We'll work on your sleeping quarters today. My son will find a way to secure a residence permit. Are you up to providing twenty-four-hour services?" Her eyes appraise my face with a judging quality. I hold still as she says, "Can you, an American executive, be content as a housekeeper? We will compensate you well."

Sitting on her silk chair, wrapped in a cashmere blanket, Madame cannot begin to understand how almost any job is preferable to wandering cold streets. I extend my hand to close the deal. This is life and death—pride is not a factor.

"Jeffrey has storage at the hospital. He will shower and eat two meals there. You won't be bothered by him."

She pulls her hand back. "The offer is for your services. I have not come to a conclusion about your husband."

"But no one can sleep in the churches alone." Her eyes leave my face as I challenge her beliefs about conditions in Paris. "There are hygiene issues and thieves. It is dangerous."

"Perhaps you have chosen the wrong shelter." Madame Lambert switches to French, speaks with authority. "Keeping documented aliens safe is a priority."

Official news stories suggest Americans trapped in France spend days touring galleries and eating at cafes. In Paris, everyone turns a blind eye to middle-class Americans' battle to stay alive. Not one building allows visitors without documentation inside for more than two hours. Classrooms keep foreign children warm while their parents form a moving mass on city streets until the churches open for sleepers.

"Please give Jeffrey a bed. He will stay healthy. I promise he will sanitize everything he touches. He can bring us the truth about what is happening in Paris."

She taps pale thin fingers together while thinking. "All right. But he must keep his distance." Madame clears her throat. "Now, I will go to the market and you must work."

Alone in Madame Lambert's apartment, I pack thin china tea cups, ancient glasses, and priceless objects. When she returns, a corner of the salon is clear for her bed. I cannot read her mind as we discuss ways to make the space more comforting. Movers will transfer her things in the morning.

Jeffrey rings the doorbell at six. His medical mask hangs loosely below a freshly shaven face and throat. He pulls off his hat. Bare scalp instead of thick dark curls jettisons me into fear. He clearly is prepared to work in a contagious environment. I almost don't recognize the smell of hospital disinfectant soap rising from his warm body.

He bends close to kiss my cheek. "Don't look so scared," he whispers. "It's standard protocol."

"Stephanie says the hospital is feeding you," Madame says as he tips his head. "Excuse me while I check our dinner."

"There were ten cases of influenza at our clinic today among Parisians with no foreigner contacts." Jeffrey keeps his voice low as Madame works in the kitchen. "All ages. I'd like to watch for news coverage. Don't look at Madame, stay calm. Any progress?"

"She's offered me a job with housing and a bed upstairs for you." Jeffrey subtly flips up one thumb while I turn on the television. A story begins about riots in Belgium where the coalition government collapsed as news spread of influenza within the country. I cry out loud as the camera catches a crowd stoning a couple with a young child. He shuts off the television.

"That will never happen here," Madame Lambert says across the room. "The French have been friends of the Americans for centuries."

I can't stop crying. The stoned woman wore shoes like the ones I left in a Paris charity box. Shoes that marked me as American and a possible carrier of the virus.

Madame appears uneasy. "Hush, Stephanie. We have much to accomplish. My son has given me directions to follow if Jeffrey is to stay here." She begins moving. "Follow me upstairs."

We walk up thick carpeted steps, down a hall past her suite and two empty bedrooms. She stops at the linen closet, opens its door, and then presses a hidden button. Another door opens.

"This will be your space, Jeffrey." Inside the compact space, bunks and shelves are lit by a blue-white flickering light. "My husband's family sheltered Jews in the war. He maintained the space as a safe room."

Not looking back, Jeffrey steps into the enclosure where hunted men and women hid generations earlier. His face is serious.

She is gracious, as if offering a plush bed. "My husband was a wealthy businessman who harbored suspicions of a dangerous future. With blankets and such it will do, no?"

"Thank you, Madame." Jeffrey turns back to us. "Stephanie and I are both grateful."

"About Stephanie." She touches my arm. "My son secured documentation within the emergency laws so you can live here openly. We will open the servant's room underneath the stairs. No mattress in the pantry."

Jeffrey bows his head. "Merci. Vous êtes un sauveur."

* * *

We begin this new phase of exile that evening by making up two single beds. After Jeffrey tours the servant's room, I help him make up a bunk in the safe room.

"I'm going to give you this for safekeeping," he says as he places his wedding band in my hand. "It's too loose these days. Wear it around your neck on a chain like we're high school sweethearts." He kisses my forehead. "I never had a girl wear my ring like that."

"My jewelry is in the airport locker." My fingers close around the ring.

"Keep it in your room then. Hospital security can't handle the crowds and the clinic is insane." His voice moves away from emotion. "I'll bring anything of value home."

Home stays sweet in my mind as I strip down to my underwear and slide between real sheets. The quiet around me is interrupted by the apartment's innocent night noises. There is no sound of strangers coughing or snoring or crying. I keep a hand on my meager bag of belongings, though there is no one here to steal it when I close my eyes. I can use the toilet without fear of a stranger grabbing my foot. Instead of comfort, I feel the isolation of closing my eyes outside the warmth of Jeffrey's arms.

In the morning he surprises me by crawling down a ladder from his safe room into a closet near the kitchen. I jump so quickly I spill hot coffee across my hand. My elegant diamond wedding band contrasts on a finger no longer manicured for boardroom presentations. Jeffrey cares for the scald while grousing about Madame's insistence that he use a rear entrance through the parking garage which will add two blocks to his walk to the metro. When he leaves, I start a list of small things to buy to bring comfort back into our lives—hand lotion, shaving cream, socks, pajamas.

"It is time we return to living like beautiful women," Madame says when she returns from shopping with more toiletries and clothing than I requested. "I will show you how to use my kitchen and turn it over to you. Once the packing is complete, we will have leisure time and will work on your poor hands and my awful whiskery chin."

In the midst of boxes and packing barrels, her expensive salon reduced to a gathering space and bedroom, a bond begins to form with this old woman. "Yes, I would like that."

Jeffrey returns that evening in clean hospital scrubs instead of street clothes and says his things are being washed with a special disinfectant. We sit on the steps to the second floor and talk about the illness tiptoeing into Paris. He tells me wealthy nonresidents are occupying protected lodging in the prestigious 16th arrondissement with private duty medical staff while the city's poor are unable to find treatment. He worries the brown trucks will fall behind on gathering victims and panic will develop.

The next day Madame and I drive to the country to find produce to freeze or preserve. On the way back we stop at every grocery to buy staples. In one shop we hear that a fire burned inside a church the previous night, killing many refugees. Parisians believe the fire was set by an American guard to hide virus carriers too sick to walk.

Later, invited into the salon, Jeffrey tells us of the creation of an American refugee camp on the outskirts of Paris. The buildings, on the fringe of public housing, had been empty for some time following the riots in 2005. At transport pickup sites, it has been arranged that medical staff will do assessments and isolate the ill.

"I read the palliative care plans for sick Americans, but didn't see any for other foreigners," Jeffrey says while resting on a settee. He wears his sterile mask as casually as a necktie or name badge. "The Army is in the process of setting up a field hospital."

"So the virus is in Paris." Madame looks at a small oil painting of two young boys.

"Yes. The epicenter appears to be open markets in the Latin Quarter." His voice sounds ragged, over-used. I know she recently shopped and dined there with a friend.

Jeffrey speaks directly to me. "Attacks on Americans are escalating. I would feel better if you didn't go out alone."

"And how are the Americans treating foreigners trapped in the United States?" Madame's question implies she knows the answer.

"I've heard of chaos in the States. There have been many deaths." Jeffrey clears his throat. "We're still waiting for news about our families."

I hear Madame crying that night. The phone has not rung for two days and she worries about her sons. In the cocoon of her apartment, neither of us sleeps. Toward morning, creaking floors track her path from bed to the toilet and back. Through the small window in my room, I see snow begin to fall.

Jeffrey is tired and barely speaks in the morning. "I could be late," he says as we hug goodbye. "I should have stayed at the hospital last night, but wanted to tell you about the situation in person. This must be how things started at home."

"Please take care of yourself. I love you." I am already adjusted to his shining skull and the medicinal smell.

"I love you, too." He pulls a stocking cap over his head and closes the door.

Madame, pale and tired, only drinks coffee for breakfast. "I think I'll take it easy today. Perhaps I've been too busy for an eighty-year-old woman." She asks for a throw and a glass of water. I bring both and we read the paper, me moving slowly through the French.

She coughs frequently. I think of calling Jeffrey. Her hand shakes when the phone rings and she reaches to pick up the receiver. I don't mean to listen to her conversation, but realize she is speaking about Jeffrey. I hear the word "missing" used a few times. I stand.

"What are you doing, Stephanie?" She coughs as she replaces the receiver.

"Getting my coat."

"No, you must stay here. Officials will arrive in a few minutes. Be sure you have your documentation." Her eyes look bright for a moment, then quickly turn dull again.

"Tell me what they said."

"When Jeffrey was fifteen minutes late for his first patient, the medical director alerted security."

"I'll need to call his parents." Someone who knows Jeffrey must know I am frightened.

"Not until we have more information. Bring me my quilted robe."

I help her into the long, silky garment. "You're burning with fever."

"Actually, I am cold." She straightens her shirt and pants. "Quite cold."

Two somber men stand outside when I answer the doorbell's buzz. "Madame Bacher, I am Pierre Champeau, head of hospital security, and this is Jonathan Belz from the U.S. embassy. I am an old friend of Madame Lambert's family and she is expecting us."

"Pierre, we have not spoken since your daughter's baptism." Madame joins us and lifts her face for light cheek kisses from the hospital representative. "Pierre attended school with my sons," she explains. "How is your family?"

I knew I must wait for their French politeness to run its course. Belz removes his gloves and adjusts his glasses. He does not look at me until Madame steps back.

"Madame Bacher, there's no need for us to come in." Belz speaks flawless French. "This will only take a minute. Dr. Bacher has been conscripted by the U.S. government for the duration of this international crisis to provide medical services to critical personnel." He stops.

Madame Lambert frowns. "Certainly your embassy has more consideration for this citizen than to deliver such important news in this manner?"

"I am sorry to be abrupt, but this is a time of great difficulty." He stuffs his hands in the pockets of his coat. "Dr. Bacher is not the only U.S. physician in Paris; there are other families to notify."

"Let me speak with Jeffrey." I speak in French, but my mind keens in English. "Tell me where he is."

Belz withdraws papers from one pocket. "I don't know that information. Here is my card and a letter. Your husband knows we will do everything within our power to keep you safe until you can be returned to the United States. There is a voicemail box where you may leave messages." Someone has written a number on the card. "This is your identification code. We will be in contact within thirty days to update you." Instead of eye contact, he tips his head. "Be brave, Madame Bacher."

Long after they walk back into the snowy morning, I remain in the foyer. My scalded hand throbs, my mind skitters through what I remember Belz saying. How could something that was merely a news story in August turn into this nightmare?

"Stephanie, please close the foyer door. Could you warm my coffee?" Under patrician tones, Madame's voice quivers. In the morning light, her face is without color. By noon she returns to bed. Her physician gives me rapid directions in French to deal with the fever and violent vomiting. He promises to deliver a medication that will ease symptoms. There is nothing else to be done. Concern that we brought the illness to Madame's home, and fear of where I would live if she died, commit me to fight for her survival.

She mumbles and becomes disoriented throughout the long day and night. At times she cries for her sons, other times grips my hands and murmurs "mère." I change her clothing, her bedding and force medicine between her lips. At daybreak I expect her to be better and am disappointed.

Just before the streetlights extinguish, a brown truck drives the narrow street, pulls over to the sidewalk, and stops three doors away. Two men hop out and carry a stretcher to the door. The virus is on our street. I dial her sons' numbers again, and again leave messages, try two phones in the States, then the American embassy number where a taped message directs me to call during regular hours.

* * *

Three days later, Madame's fever breaks, but I am not sure of her future. As a feeble winter dawn begins, I wipe her face and upper body with a wet washcloth, carefully hold a glass of water to her cracked lips, and will her to stay alive. By the time she returns to sleep, the French government indefinitely closes its borders. The brown truck drives past without stopping. I sit next to the window, feeling like a castaway. She whispers my name from across the room.

"What do you need, Madame?" French is her language and has become mine.

"I am going to die. Call my sons."

"You are not going to die. But we will call to let them know that you are better."

"Try them now. I must speak with them before I die." She coughs, a painful hammering sound from her thin chest. I don't tell her of my fear that her sons' phones ring in now-empty homes.

"You've come through the worst, Madame." I tuck a pillow into her arms. "Hold this when you cough."

She accepts the pillow, coughs again, moans. "This is how my life is going to end. I lived through world war and the Depression. Did I die when I buried my daughter or my husband? No, not until

I am alone does death come for me." Her voice breaks down into a frail whisper. "Do not let them put me in one of those death trucks. I do not want to burn with strangers."

"Hush, you must think good thoughts. Let me help you into your chair, then I will try your sons again." I hope she will tire and not put me through the useless dialing.

She walks with minimal assistance, the hope of a talk with her sons acting as fuel to push her weakened body. The first call rings without answer, but her oldest son answers when I dial the second number, and I fight emotion while telling him that she is better.

They speak. I walk to the windows to give them privacy. Behind me Madame cries softly as she tires from the work of talking so long. Lights begin showing through the drawn drapes of neighbors. I think of eating breakfast with Jeffrey in our home in Chicago, wonder what is left of our country and that faraway life.

"Stephanie." I turn as she says my name. "Jean says there are problems with the Paris phone lines, but if you give him your families' numbers, he will make calls."

"How is my mother really doing?" he asks before I can speak.

"She has come through the worst and has my full devotion. She is all I have in Paris."

"Thank you."

"There are three numbers I would like you to try if that is not too much to ask."

"All in America?"

"Yes, in Chicago, Minneapolis, Philadelphia."

"Madame Bacher, I will do my best, but I won't sugarcoat the situation. There have been many deaths and many systems have disintegrated. People will not leave their houses for any reason, including work."

Madame bends her head, coughs out a string of phlegm, too weak to even wipe it from her chin. I ask him to hold on while I clean her. He talks over my words.

"Be patient, Madame Bacher. This may take many days." His voice hints that his efforts might be wasted. "If my mother takes a turn, call me and we will talk further." He says something to another person and I hear a dog whining in his world. His attention returns to our conversation. "If there is nothing else, God bless you." The line falls silent.

Later today I will take money from Madame's purse and tie her scarf around my head. I will pull on the good rubberized European boots Jeffrey found in an abandoned automobile. I will go out into the neighborhood as a French woman's housekeeper in search of bread and butter and eggs. I will survive.

We Are Still Feeling

Karen Bovenmyer

Outer perimeter breached. Stop.

    Nicht and Onyango zeroed. Stop.

    Machines coming. Stop.

    Request evac. Stop.

    Machines coming. Machines coming. Machines coming.

    "Stop," I say, smoothing Asya's braids back from her forehead and tucking them behind her ear. They are greasy with fear-sweat and worse, and leave an oily residue on my fingers. "That's enough."

    The last mobile member of my ten *decem*, Asya, my translator, holds the com strands gently in her long, brown fingers. The pink cuticles of her nails have only just started to gray—she has another week, maybe two, before her nails fall out. Her eyes are burnt up, but her hearing and sense of touch are still excellent. We wait together for Command's answer to come stuttering down the filaments, the faint clanging of the machines battering the outer door echoing inside the bunker like a metal heartbeat.

    I'm no great shakes at waiting, never have been, and we dropped to this bunker to gather intel, so that's what I want to do.

    I dip my fingers back into the brain jar, knuckles tingling as cold gray matter slides past them, and use its power to boost out to the distant remains of my *decem*. Nicht is dark, but Onyango, though he's been zeroed to a limbless trunk, still has eyes, so I look through them. Two scout machines work over the access door, jackhammering with precision. Nicht is bones and smoking char beside them and I see Onyango's left boot and shattered shin on the ground nearby. Onyango moans under my continued invasion as we join fully, and one of the robot scouts—a former auto-assembler now fitted with the control module we were sent to retrieve—stops jackhammering. The last thing we see through Onyango's eyes is the business end of Scout Two's pounder. I pull out before we feel it pulp his face. Only Asya and me now—and none of the intel on the machines' plans that Command wanted.

"Kummer, are we zeroed?" Asya's vocals still work too. She sounds younger than she looks. She was about thirty when she died but she sounds like a teen. Sometimes they regress like that when awakened. You can only rise people you've known in life—people you've had a personal connection with. Using another empath's brain in a jar to make lovers and family and friends and coworkers get up and serve make empaths like me useful—even after we're dead. How many lovers' bodies do I have left before I'm jarred? Does it even matter?

"Not yet." I try to make the lie hopeful. We have maybe five minutes before the scouts get through. There isn't jack or shit Command can do in that time—at least the scouts haven't found and severed the bio-fibers so we still have coms.

As if summoned by that thought, they move. Asya jumps in her chair, surprised by the sudden twitching of the filaments resting in her hands, and repeats Command's answer back to me.

Do not drop your puppets. Stop.

Decem Tray incoming. Stop.

Preserve the jar at all costs. Repeat.

Preserve the jar. Stop.

"See, it'll be all right," I tell her, and her shoulders relax. But I don't hear the rotors of a stripped-to-analog CH-47 Chinook helicopter dropping in a *decem* like the one that brought us—I only hear the clanging of the scouts on the door. Anything digital the machines own, much like we own the dead and the bio-filaments grown to communicate with the head puppeteer at Command. I slide my other hand into the jar and reach, focusing to push my range to the wavering, migraine edge. There is nothing dead but Asya in range, no other *decem* of ten with a puppeteer and her jar. "Tell them I've got nothing."

The clanging intensifies, then stops with a mighty squeal of protesting metal. The scouts are in. We have maybe a few more minutes while they move tactically down the tunnels and find us.

"Take me." Asya drops the Command filaments. "Preserve the jar." She reaches dead hands to me, as if she can pull me into her, instead of the other way around.

I want to smooth my ex-lover's braids back from her forehead again and kiss it lightly, but instead I grip the jar's gray matter with both hands and push my consciousness into her. What is left of Asya is so light—the long-forgotten taste of lemons on the back of my tongue. She's someone who should have lived.

We need to use my eyes, Kummer's eyes, because Asya has none, so our movements are awkward and uncoordinated. We pick up the cannon that's too big for either of us to use safely, slip Asya's skinny arms through the straps, and tighten the chest harness. We station ourselves in front of the door, wedging our small body inside a metal locker to moderate the kickback, so we can fire until our meat gives out.

The pounding on the interior hatch starts. Dirt and dust shower down from seams in the metal bunker we never realized were there. We make sure the ammo belt is clear so we can fire and fire and fire until there is nothing left.

The filaments twitch on the floor, but there is no translator to tell us what Command is saying. We want to say:

Bunker taken. Stop.

Kummer and Asya zeroed. Stop.

Stop. Stop. Oh God. Stop.

The scouts break through, and we let loose with the cannon, screaming, Asya's too-young voice and mine, Kummer's, twining until the cannon crushes our lungs and we can't use Asya's air, so it is only Kummer screaming, but we can't hear it over the gunfire. We pull the trigger and keep pulling. We cut one of the scouts in two, its legs scissoring without control, the heavy upper body and jackhammer kiltering over, pounding the floor.

Then we hear the rotors and feel the other puppeteer arrive with her *decem*, too late, because the second scout is already on us, on Asya, bending the cannon's red-hot barrel even as we fire and shatter ourselves. The scout pulps our face, Asya's beloved face, and I stay to feel it, we will always feel it, we are still feeling it.

The scout drops Asya's body and comes for us, as Kummer's limbs jerk with the shock of Asya's zeroing. I ride the waves, both of Kummer's hands, my hands, our hands, in the jar, clutching, clutching.

The other dead—Tray's *decem*—rush into the bunker, swarming the scout, even as it reaches us and jackhammers Kummer's leg, my leg. Ours? I fall, the jar hanging from my hands, Kummer's hands. But there are too many bodies on the robot, too many targets to pulp. The scout can't reach Kummer through the other *decem*. One of them opens fire, cutting the scout, cutting the *decem* to bloody, oily shreds.

"Goddamn," the other puppeteer says. Her left pocket reads TRAY. She's short and blonde with a prosthetic arm, but the other is in her own jar, fingering the empathic gray matter. Two big men with chest cannons flank her, ammo belts looping away into backpacks. Tray comes into the bunker, looks at the shuddering, crawling remains of her *decem*, and mine, which is only me, us, the ghost of lemons, Kummer. The scouts both still whine and whir but are in too many pieces. Unlike us, they don't get back up even when they are shattered. "Kummer?"

We cannot answer her. We are still feeling Asya, who is gone. The puppeteer reads the name on our uniform and answers her own question. The command filaments twitch on the floor, and her interpreter, a round-faced boy with almond-shaped eyes and a black ponytail, rushes forward to take the messages. Tray removes the robot's data module—the information we'd been sent to get in the first place—and shoves it in the boy's backpack.

"Tell them we have a module and the jar. The puppeteer is whole," she says.

But she is wrong. We are not whole. We will never be whole again.

Tray brushes our hair back from our forehead and tucks the strands behind our ear as the helicopter lifts the remains of her *decem* and our jar, our body, Kummer's leg splinted and bound, up and away from the compromised bunker. They will take us back to base, and they will fit us with a new *decem* of various dead acquaintances—no shortage of bodies since the machines started eliminating us—but we will never really leave the bunker. We are here forever, fear-sweat oily on our fingers, the taste of lemons on our tongue, and a too-young voice asking, "Kummer, are we zeroed?"

Yes, Asya, we were. We are.

Stop.

Unpleasantness at 20,000 Feet

Terry Faust

Co-pilot Arnold Kenneth knew the flight would be strange the moment the William Shatner fan club stepped onboard. The group, stuffed into various homemade *Star Trek* costumes, took up half the coach section. In the forward exit door, Arnold and Captain William Hynek greeted them and suffered requests to come about, beam up, beam down, check the captain's log, and fire the forward phasers. Arnold admired the captain's good-natured calm. It was Arnie's first flight riding shotgun with the venerable Captain Hynek, Gold Star Airway's most senior pilot. He was a model for solid flying skills. His miraculous landing decades ago of an engine-damaged turbo-prop, a Lockheed Constellation, had earned him mythical status among pilots. The high-spirited and rather abusive passengers had no way of knowing that. To Arnie, it was an honor to fly with him—and something of a surprise.

Leveling out at 20,000 feet, Arnie checked their flight plan. Everything was on schedule. The Boeing's powerful jet engines purred. The stars were out and the weather looked perfect all the way to Chicago. He relaxed. The captain seemed preoccupied with scribbling in a blue three-ringed binder and Arnie was reluctant to strike up a casual conversation. The captain was old enough to be his father but he had the vigor of a man half his age. And he had requested this drab Las Vegas to Chicago run with Arnie, a complete break from the exotic overseas flights such a senior pilot would normally command. Arnie couldn't account for it. He leaned back, easing his neck muscles, and set the aircraft to autopilot. The unmoving pinpoints of starlight burned brightly.

Out of the corner of Arnie's right eye he caught movement—beyond the windscreen. It was brief, an instant, more like a flash. He checked the cockpit for anything that might have caused a reflection. Nothing. It must have been outside... or his imagination playing tricks. There, again, he saw something in front of the starboard wing. He leaned forward, craning to see out the windshield. A car-shaped silhouette blocked the stars. It was hard to judge its distance or shape. There! The plane's belly strobe reflected off a brightly colored object. The afterimage of a car registered on his retina. It was close, real close. The plane's strobes flicked a microsecond, illuminating it again. Arnie pinched his eyes and rubbed them. It looked for all the world like the little clown car he remembered from his hometown circus.

"Ah, Captain?"

"Hmmm?" Hynek murmured, still deep into his notebook. He appeared to be drawing.

Arnie hesitated. The car was still there, taking up a position just forward and to one side of the right engine. Dim light from the cabin windows illuminated it. It didn't have wings or rockets or any means of propulsion. It was an impossibility. If Arnie told the captain what he saw he'd sound crazy. Arnie's flying career was already on the edge. He'd gone on record a month ago claiming a triangular UFO had buzzed his plane. It had been broad daylight and the thing had sped past, climbing at an unbelievable speed. Though his crew had pleaded with him to forget it, he'd reported it. The result was counseling and an unspoken demotion to strictly domestic flights. Recording UFOs was frowned upon. But the car was still there. If he was hallucinating, it was a very solid-looking hallucination, one that was close to being sucked into number two engine.

"Something wrong, Arnie?" Captain Hynek asked. His baritone voice exuded warmth and confidence… a fatherly voice, a voice that wouldn't judge.

"I'm not sure, Captain," Arnie said. His voice trembled. The airline's psychiatrist had, in so many words, warned Arnold that another UFO sighting would ground him.

"Is it the clown car?" Hynek asked.

Arnie blinked in disbelief. Had the captain said 'clown car?' To be safe he asked, "Clown car?"

Captain Hynek set his binder down, unbuckled, and leaned across Arnie to catch a glimpse of the comic little car. "Hmph. It's a sight, all right."

"You see it too?"

"Definitely not." Hynek returned to his seat and buckled in. "Isn't there. Never was there. Never could be."

Arnie took a deep breath. Was Hynek joking? Arnie didn't think so. Was this some kind of bizarre test? Arnie didn't know what to do.

The captain seemed to know the inner turmoil his co-pilot was going through and he patted Arnie's shoulder. Turning the blue three-ring binder so Arnie could see it, he showed Arnie a remarkably accurate sketch of the car. "We picked it up over Omaha. It's been on my side, off number one, for the last ten minutes." Hynek handed Arnie his book so he could take a closer look.

Arnie's mouth opened, then closed. The captain had all the details, right down to the foxtail on the antenna. A brief summary of their altitude, location, time, and weather conditions accompanied the drawing.

"Ahh, er." It was all Arnie could manage.

Hynek chuckled. "It's a real beauty. Haven't seen anything like it for, oh, thirty years." Hynek leaned over and thumbed back in the rather thick collection of pages. Arnie looked on with growing alarm as the veteran pilot leafed past sketches of saucer-shaped objects, past cigar-shaped and triangular drawings, then settled on a few pages of farm machinery. He tapped his finger on a manure spreader and chuckled to himself. Arnie didn't dare ask. Hynek ended in a section of outdated automobiles. The paper was slightly yellowed with age. The captain pointed to an ancient VW bug. "Closest thing but not quite; same clown car motif though. I'd say the thing out there's more of a Mini Cooper."

Too stunned to comment, Arnie leaned back in his seat. What could he say?

A hesitant knock at the cockpit door was followed by a pert young stewardess's face. "Captain, I'm sorry to bother you. I know this will sound silly but some passengers claim... well, they say there's something off the starboard side of the plane... a little car, like a Volkswagen Bug?" The stewardess gave a little laugh. Her eyes darted back and forth between the pilot and co-pilot, hoping for a surprised reaction and possibly a rational explanation. The captain smiled back confidently. Arnie simply returned her amazed gaze with a look of dumb disbelief. Melissa had flown with Arnie once before and never with Hynek, as far as Arnie knew. She'd always seemed competent and rational.

When he and the captain didn't so much as raise an eyebrow she cleared her throat nervously and asked, "What should I tell them?"

Hynek slapped the blue book shut and smiled reassuringly. "Tell them it's a Mini Cooper." He stretched to look out the right side window and nodded to himself. "I'd say a '98. What do you think, Arnie?"

Arnold looked up at the stewardess with a panicky expression. The stewardess took a step back. He sensed that only he and the stewardess saw the insanity of the situation.

Hynek chuckled, delighted by his own mirth. "We're just joking, of course."

The stewardess's eyes widened at this obvious lie. "Of course," she said and continued to look at them both for some shred of guidance. "Captain, I should tell them something. They are pretty upset."

"Sorry, Melissa. You tell our esteemed passengers we're passing through high altitude swamp gas."

Melissa's mouth opened in question. The captain held out a finger, urging her to pull it. "Get it? Passing gas?" Melissa made no move to pull the proffered finger. If Arnie didn't know better he'd think the captain was teasing Melissa, enjoying some weird game. But the next instant the captain sobered up and sighed. "Serious, serious, serious. Okay, tell them we're experiencing mild electromagnetic fluctuations. It's causing vortex optical distortions similar to St. Elmo's fire." The captain pressed his bushy eyebrows together and adopted a serious expression. "Tell them it's nothing to worry about."

Melissa looked doubtful.

The captain grabbed the intra-plane microphone. "I'll get on the intercom and make an announcement if you'd like."

"No!" Melissa nearly shouted. "No, sir, I'll handle it." She left quickly, relieved to return to her passengers.

"She's a new one," Hynek said and jerked his thumb in the direction Melissa had fled. He returned to his seat and buckled in. "Some of the older stewies will talk to her. She'll be okay. No sense of humor though. Got to have a sense of humor up here. And a sense of proportion."

Arnold leaned closer to the captain and asked in almost a whisper, "Captain?"

"What, Arnie?"

"What are vortex optical distortions?"

"How the hell should I know? Made it up. It sure sounded good." The captain tucked his blue binder into his flight case and looked up. At Arnie's surprised frown, the Captain said, "You're wondering about all this." He tapped his book, "My sketches? Merely a hobby."

"But…"

Hynek held up a hand to stop further comment. "I've been flying forty years, Arnie, my boy. How long do you think I'd have my license if I complained every time there was a friggin' UFO flying alongside? I'd be flying a padded cell, not this plane. You understand?"

Arnie grimaced and nodded. He understood only too well.

"Now, if you want to radio anything in, be my guest. But my advice is to forget it." The captain's gaze burned right into him.

It ran against Arnie's nature to lie, but the company doctor had made it clear that more flying saucer reports weren't welcome. Arnie nodded. "I guess it's a distortion."

Captain Hynek patted him on the shoulder. "Good man."

A slight tremor passed through the plane. The "distortion" rested on the wing, parked as if it were on a city street. Half a dozen clowns rolled and bounced out. Two held sledgehammers. Three pulled out tin snips. And one hefted a large pickaxe and eyed the number two engine. Arnie took them for clowns, though their suits were furry and their faces were hideously contorted. Even in the cockpit, Arnie could hear the cries of consternation from the coach section.

"Dammit! Not again," Hynek said. He'd unbuckled and was staring at the clowns beside Arnie.

"Again?"

Hynek nodded to himself. "Clown gremlins!" He said it with the assurance that there could be no other answer. "How many would you say?"

"Six," Arnie counted. "One's about to… he's taking a pickaxe to the engine!"

"Hold on," the captain said, and hopped back behind the controls. With a twist of the control yoke the right wing dipped. The gremlins tottered, off balance. Helpless, they watched their little car slide off the wing and disappear into the blackness. Hynek increased the roll and two figures tumbled after their vehicle. The rest sprawled on the wing, spread-eagled, and clawed at the seamless aluminum surface. Slowly they slithered toward the wingtip.

"Caaaa caa captain!" was all Arnie could say.

"Arnie, get a grip." Hynek's well-modulated baritone was like a slap in the face. "How we doing out there?"

"Whaaa?" Arnie's eyes were fixed on the last clown who chucked his pickaxe in a futile attempt to grab an aileron with both hands.

"Any left?"

"One."

Hynek turned the yoke left then right. The plane responded sluggishly, but the wing rose and fell. The furry clown plunged into the abyss.

"That do it?"

"Yes, sir."

"Good. I hate those things. My advice: never let gremlins on your wingtip, Arnie. Never."

"Yes, sir."

"Take the stick, please."

Arnie could not tear his eyes off the empty expanse of aluminum.

"Arnie, take over," the captain commanded. "Get us back on course."

"Yes, sir." Arnie reluctantly grasped the yoke and put his eyes forward. His training kicked in and he checked the plane's vital systems. What had just happened could not have happened. The unreality of it almost made it too real. He welcomed the touch of the controls and the solidity of the cockpit. His heart was racing and he gulped, trying to steady himself. Hynek pulled out his blue book, opened it and made a note. Pen in hand, he looked at Arnie, studied him for several seconds. "You all right, Arnie?"

"Yep," Arnie said. His 'yep' was as solid as Jell-O and two octaves higher than normal.

"You realize none of this happened?" Hynek said. It wasn't a question.

"It didn't?"

"No, it didn't."

Arnie returned the captain's penetrating gaze. His earlier question of why the celebrity veteran Gold Star pilot was sitting beside him now had a murky answer. "Captain. Is this why you requested this flight?"

Hynek smiled and nodded. "You're a good pilot, Arnie."

"You expected the little car?"

"Let's say I wasn't surprised. Gold Star Airways has been worried about you, Arnie. They think you are seeing things."

"But... but..."

"Did you see anything?"

Arnie gripped the yoke and then eased up. It started to make sense. "No. I guess not."

"That's good, Arnie, very good. I'm going to tell them you're all right. We'd hate to lose a good pilot." The captain patted his shoulder and tapped his blue book. "Off the record, a word of advice. Start your own book. Some pilots find that it helps."

Every Thing in Its Place

Lyda Morehouse

The thing watched Andrea from every corner of every room.

Though technically an 'it,' Andrea thought of the thing as a he. She wasn't sure why. There was no real indication of gender, except perhaps a lack of breasts and a muscular upper body. Surely she was anthropomorphising the thing. But the thing had power and that power frightened her; therefore, it was male.

Right now, the thing lounged in the corner, pretending to be harmless. Susan didn't seem to see it. She was talking on and on about her newest beau, some guy named Denis from the office. Andrea nodded and 'uh-huh'ed in the appropriate places, but her concentration was focused on the thing.

Dark wings hugged a sleek black body. He blended to near invisibility in the long shadows the afternoon sun threw against the living room wall. Breath came and went like the hiss of the radiator. Arms, crossed over his barrel chest, moved ever so slightly with each faux snore. His eyes were nearly shut, as though he were sleeping, but Andrea could see the golden glow of his watchful stare beneath veiled lashes.

He always watched her.

She'd tried to get rid of him with salt and a banishing spell, but he clung stubbornly to His Place, because he was the Thing of this Place.

At least that was what he'd said when he first appeared Halloween night. Andrea had been preparing for a solitary ritual on Samhain, the pagan New Year. She'd wanted everything to be perfect and everything felt so right. The dark moon, Hecate's moon, cast not even a sliver of a reflection on this magical day and she was bleeding as if in tune with the Goddess Herself. Andrea had rushed home from work and immediately started cleaning and purifying her small Uptown apartment.

At each corner she'd blown some sage smoke into the air and whispered, "Everything has its place."

Closing her eyes, she'd imagined a thread spiraling down from the moon, like an ebony spider's web. Andrea could almost feel its feathery touch as it danced across her chakra. Dark moon energy had filled her. Smiling to herself, she couldn't wait to set up her altar. The way things were going tonight, she would be the Goddess Incarnate this time, for real.

She'd been halfway around the room with her smudge stick when he'd said, "I am the Thing of this Place."

His voice had startled her. Its deep, resonant baritone, like the horn of a passing light rail train, broke her mantra. That's when she'd realized she'd been saying it wrong. Somewhere between the kitchen and the living room, she'd blown a synapse—lost her mind, mixed her words up. As she stared into the blue-black face of this winged beast, she heard herself saying: "Every place has its Thing."

He was that thing, the one that belonged to this place. In a way, it made sense. Though the apartment had felt instantly like home with its gleaming hardwood floors and large windows, some uneasy thing had always crept around the edges of her consciousness. Even before the thing had materialized, something dark, something shadowy, haunted the angle of each wall. That's why she'd concentrated so much magic into the corners that Halloween. She'd wanted to keep everything in its place. Instead, she'd conjured the very thing of the place.

"Did you say something?" Susan's lips were taut with worry.

"I'm sorry." Andrea put on an apologetic smile, dragging her eyes from the thing. "I was just thinking about some things I need to take care of."

The thing roused, stretching out its long body. The creaks of his bones sounded like the shaking tree branches in the November wind.

"Okay, well... maybe I should go," Susan said, looking around for her coat.

"No, don't! Not yet. I'm sorry, I guess I'm just a little tired from work. Can't I make you one last cup of hot chocolate before you go?"

Susan smiled. It was a thin sort of smile, and Andrea knew Susan would stay a moment longer, but only out of pity. Everyone at the office thought Andrea was 'weird AF,' Susan included. But Susan liked to talk and Andrea would listen. They weren't friends, not really. Andrea didn't have real friends. Even so, Andrea didn't want to be alone with the thing. Not yet.

"Okay, one more cup," Susan said, as she followed Andrea into the tiny kitchen.

Andrea started the gas flame under the kettle and tried to remember the last thread of Susan's monologue. "Do you really think it will be okay to date someone at work?"

"Eh, we're not in the same department." Susan shrugged. Leaning against the doorway, her golden hair caught the fluorescent light. Behind her, the thing moved across the floor to the opposite corner. Eyes, reflecting like a cat's, watched them from the dining room now. Susan said, "I never hear you talk about anyone, Andrea."

"I'm an independent woman, who likes her Place to Herself." Her eyes locked on the thing, just beyond Susan's shoulder. "I've told you that already."

"Don't you get lonely, being all alone in this big place?"

The thing's shadowy face cracked with a toothy grin. His fangs were startlingly white against his dark features. Andrea snorted an almost wistful laugh. "Alone?"

Susan's eyes searched Andrea's face for something. "Yes. Alone. Doesn't it get lonely?"

How could Andrea be lonely? He was there every morning when she woke up. Yellow eyes danced in the morning sun—watching. The thing's eyes followed her to the bathroom, to the kitchen, to the living room. She heard his rustling steps, like autumn leaves, behind her everywhere in the apartment. She would kill to be alone.

"I'm not lonely," Andrea said absently. "I have things to amuse me."

As if enjoying the private joke, the thing blinked at her sleepily. He extended his sable wings along the wall, settling into His Place.

He will never leave, Andrea told herself. She had to do something about him tonight.

Susan cleared her throat. "You should really get out more often."

"Oh, I know," Andrea said agreeably.

"Maybe… maybe you and I could go to that new bar downtown sometime," Susan offered. "Denis knows a lot of nice guys. I'm sure you'd have fun once we got there."

And have all the men staring with the thing's hungry look? "Oh, I don't think so."

Susan frowned. "Well, maybe sometime."

"Yes," Andrea said, remembering herself. "Thanks for the offer. Really."

Susan looked meaningfully at the clock on the kitchen wall. "Oh, is that the time? Sorry. I really need to head out."

"Okay." This time Andrea didn't protest. "Thanks for coming by."

"Sure," Susan said. Reaching for her coat, Susan leaned against the wood molding. Her hand rested inches away from the thing's broad chest. Andrea held her breath, but the thing paid no attention to Susan.

Shrugging into her coat, Susan asked, "You okay? You look like you've seen a ghost."

Andrea pulled her hands away from her mouth and let out the breath she'd been holding.

The thing yawned.

"Andrea?"

"I don't want to keep you," Andrea whispered.

"Um…" Susan hesitated for a moment. She followed Andrea's gaze to where the thing lounged against the wall. Then, she said, "Okay, well. See you Monday."

With that, Susan left. Andrea could hear the screen door bounce back against its frame at the bottom of the stairs, followed by the slam of the heavy wooden door. She knew the polite thing to do would have been to walk Susan out, but Andrea couldn't face coming that close to the thing. Instead, she continued to stare at him. His blue-black face returned her look impassively.

"I don't, you know," Andrea said finally. "I don't want to keep you."

"I'm not a Thing to be Kept," he agreed with a sniff. His voice rumbled like an engine springing to life. He combed his sleek fur with a taloned hand, as if offended by her suggestion, and added, "There is a hierarchy of Things, and I am a Place Thing, not a Kept Thing."

"There are more kinds of Things?" Andrea looked around the room nervously, wondering if she had any of these Kept Things lurking about.

"Hundreds."

Hundreds, thousands of things. All of them, watching, Andrea thought with a little whimper. Invisible things closing in on her, crowding her. She hardly had any room to breathe with all these things. Shutting her eyes, she could feel the pressure of all the things in her life. She batted at her hair, trying to shake off the things that clung to her. "Why don't you just go away and leave me alone?" In a hoarse whisper, she added to the rest of the room: "All of you."

The room was silent in reply. With her eyes still squeezed shut, Andrea imagined all the things gone. If she could imagine them into existence, maybe she could imagine them gone. With renewed confidence, she shouted, "You will leave, Thing of This Place and take all your Things with you."

Andrea counted to ten. As she ticked off the numbers silently, she visualized the thing spreading his wings and flying out the window. She tried to conjure the same kind of power that she had when the thing first appeared, but a small buzz, a tingle in her third eye was all she felt.

Slowly, afraid that it didn't work, Andrea opened her eyes. The thing stood by the archway. Holding his wings close to his body, he looked smaller. His lips were turned down in a frown and his eyes watched the floor.

The high-pitched whine of the teakettle's whistle startled Andrea. Swallowing hard, she turned away from the thing and ran into the kitchen. Her fingers fumbled clumsily with the knob, switching off the gas.

He was so intrusive, this Place Thing. Here to stay, he'd said. Maybe he was just like those men to whom Susan wanted so desperately to introduce her—welcomed in once, only to stay forever. Wanting Things. Andrea shivered.

Andrea crept back into her living room, hoping to sneak by the thing to her bedroom.

"Why do you want to banish me?" The thing's voice was sad, but insistent, like crickets calling in the twilight.

Gathering her courage, Andrea shouted, "This is my place!"

"Yes." His voice was soft, like tree leaves shuffling in a light breeze. "This is your Place and I am the Thing of the Place. Don't you see? We are meant to be together, always. The Goddess has seen to your happiness."

"It was the dark face of the Goddess that summoned you," Andrea reminded the thing. "She Who Destroys."

"She Who Destroys, always rebuilds. Death becomes Rebirth."

"I don't care." Andrea shook her head, banishing the confusing emotions warring within her. She had to stay focused. If she had any sympathy for the thing, she could never kill him. "I don't want you here."

"Then why did you call me?" His voice was a hiss of tires on asphalt.

"It was an accident." Her voice was almost a whimper.

"Oh." The thing's voice was low, quiet. Andrea could see she'd wounded him. His proud, handsome face crumbled just a little.

As she slipped past him, Andrea snarled cruelly. "I wish I could undo things I've done."

"But I love you as I love this Place."

Andrea frowned. Love? Love was the clingiest thing of all. Still, it might be nice to have someone to love her. She'd lied to Susan. It did get lonely in the apartment sometimes. If the lease had allowed it, she would have gotten a cat. Surely, there was no provision in her lease against Place Things. With a laugh at her own cleverness, she walked back into the kitchen and poured herself the cup of hot chocolate intended for Susan.

Strolling back into the living room, she found the thing nestled on the couch. Curled up upon himself, he looked like a black ball of dust. He seemed to be taking her rejection pretty hard. Andrea cautiously moved over to the couch. She could see the thing's shoulders shaking.

"Oh, don't cry," she said, sitting down next to him. Cautiously, she reached out and touched the ebony wings. The softness of his fur surprised her. Silky and smooth, it reminded Andrea of angora.

His shivering stopped at her touch, and his breathing evened out. Andrea had no idea she meant so much to him. She supposed it might be all right to live with a thing that loved her, especially one so soft and warm. He could keep her company while she knitted. Maybe they could talk and play cards. Then he could be the Thing of a Happy Place; maybe it would change him—make him easier to look at, less frightening.

"Hey, Thing," she said softly, still stroking his soft fur. "It's okay. I'm sorry about what I said."

He shifted slightly at her words, relaxing. His breath came in contented little huffs now as he fell asleep on the couch.

Outside, things grew dark. Shadows stretched and grew, shifting into frightening things.

* * *

Things crawled out of the woodwork—literally. Every eye or beak imagined in a knothole materialized into a Wood Thing. Kept Things clung to her, demanding attention. Andrea tried to brush things off her skirt, but they were like sandburs; she finished one section only to find more things holding tightly somewhere else. "Get away!" she screamed, "Leave me alone!"

* * *

Andrea jolted awake, sweat clinging to her body like the tiny claws of the Kept Things. She leaped out of bed and pulled at the covers. Searching for things, she stripped the bed to its sheets. Her heart pounded in her ears. The things continued to smother the breath from her.

Hugging her arms close to her chest, Andrea took a deep breath. She forced herself to breathe in and out. Finally her heartbeat steadied and she could feel the chill of the hardwood floor seeping into her toes.

She knelt down to gather up the covers.

Lifting the blanket, she gasped. The beady eyes of a Wood Thing stared up at her. Andrea jumped away in fright. She scanned the floor; she could see them crawling everywhere, through the grain of the wood. Long, thin bodies oozed over one another, clutching with scaly claws and gasping with wide-open maws.

In the bookcase, Andrea saw the face of a woman screaming. In the windowpanes, Wood Thing whispered to her. The long-faced one in the door scowled its displeasure. Its skeletal hands reached for the doorknob to lock her in.

"No!" she screamed, dashing for the door. Andrea stumbled out into the living room, where the Thing of the Place oozed out of the shadows in the couch. His glowing yellow eyes were owly with sleep. He blinked at her.

"Andrea?" Her name howled from his lips like an autumn windstorm screeching around gables.

She backed away from him in fright. All these things, she thought desperately, he brought them all here. He pretended to be gentle with her, but she knew better. He would use His Place for His Things. She'd be smothered. Things would cling to her every inch, unshakable, like ebony leeches.

"Leave this Place!" she shouted, though she knew it was useless. He was stretching out now. His body becoming the thin line where the walls met, filling the cracks with his blackness. Andrea continued backing away, until she was all the way into the kitchen and her elbow brought the teakettle to the floor with a crash.

"Andrea?" The thing's voice grated on her ears, like dogs barking in the night, building one yelp upon another in warning.

She had to kill them.

She had to destroy every Thing that threatened to smother her.

The kettle's polished steel glinted in the moonlight. A plan sprung into her desperate mind.

Turning on the gas, but not igniting the stove, Andrea smiled triumphantly.

No Thing would smother her; she would smother Every Thing.

The Last Choice

Steve McEllistrem

"Here's the bottom line," Dr. Simpson said, "you're dying."

"There must be some mistake," Senator Daniel Frederick Massico IV replied, his body shivering in its hospital gown. "Dr. Wells told me that if I allowed him to put all these nano-technology things in my body, they would give him enough warning that he could cure me of anything."

Dr. Simpson shook his head. "I'm sure what Dr. Wells said was that he could cure you of anything curable. Unfortunately, this type of cancer is very aggressive."

"But I feel fine." Actually that wasn't true. He felt nauseated. He couldn't say whether the feeling came from hearing the diagnosis or from the underlying illness, but he feared it derived from the cancer. He'd felt lousy for three days last week. He'd even considered calling Dr. Wells, but then he started to feel better. Two days ago his nanobots had sent out an alert and an appointment had been scheduled for him with Dr. Wells, who, without even seeing him, referred him to Dr. Simpson, supposedly the finest oncologist in town.

Dr. Simpson smiled sadly. "You'll have good days and bad, but the bad days will eventually outnumber the good ones. At some point we'll have to look into managing the pain. There are a number of good new options for that."

"So that's it? You're just giving up? What about a second opinion?"

"I encourage you to get a second opinion, and a third. There may be treatment options I'm not aware of, but I don't think you should get your hopes too high. My office manager can get you a list of oncologists who specialize in rare cases. And I'll make sure you've got all the information we talked about today. I know this is a lot to process."

Daniel shook his head. He felt the urge to punch somebody. "So what was the point of all this technology they put inside me?"

Dr. Simpson shrugged. "Well, it allowed us to catch your cancer at a very early stage. That buys us a lot more time to manage the disease."

"To manage my death?"

"Without it, you might have gone several more weeks before calling us. That would have limited what we can do a great deal."

"But the bottom line is, I'm still going to die."

"I wish I had better news, senator. Get more opinions, by all means, but I suggest we begin treating the symptoms immediately."

Dr. Simpson leaned forward and peered at him, expecting a response.

"Of course," Daniel said.

"Good. I'll write a prescription for a cocktail of pills, which will include Alectinib, Pembrolizumab and Docetaxel, among others. The research I've found shows that this combination has proven fairly effective at slowing the advance of this particular disease. And of course I'll continue to research it for you, see what I can find."

Left alone to dress, Daniel decided Dr. Simpson was a quack. He couldn't have cancer. He had no family history of it, particularly not something as rare as this whatever-it-was. He couldn't even pronounce it. Metastasized lung cancer: those were the only words he understood.

Spotting his aide Rebecca in the lobby, seeing the look on her face and understanding that she had somehow intuited the truth, he nearly broke down. Instead she did, throwing herself into his arms and hugging him fiercely.

"Oh, Freddy," she said.

"It'll be all right," he found himself saying, knowing how idiotic that sounded. He couldn't help but notice the lilac perfume she wore. She knew it was his favorite. How had he not detected that on the way here?

They spent twenty minutes with the nurses, getting all the information they needed about the disease and its various treatments, the side effects and the surgical options, which were none.

As the week passed, he discovered that the pills made him feel terrible, alternately nauseated and exhausted. He struggled to maintain a normal routine at the office. Rebecca was the only one he trusted with his diagnosis for now. Three more doctor visits brought complete verification of Dr. Simpson's diagnosis.

He thought about calling his ex-wife, telling her the news, but he wasn't sure how she'd take it, if she'd actually be happy he was dying, so he did nothing except schedule a follow-up appointment with Dr. Simpson.

Another test. More verification that the disease was spreading rapidly despite the medication.

"This is troubling," Dr. Simpson said. "We usually have better results than this with the drugs."

"How much time do I have?"

"A few months. Unless…"

"Unless what?"

Dr. Simpson shrugged. "I hesitate to bring it up since I know how principled you are and that you're completely opposed to it."

"Opposed to what?"

"And of course there are no guarantees. It's an experimental procedure, although the results have been promising to date."

"What procedure?" Daniel asked, his frustration mounting.

"The Jellyfish Treatment."

Revulsion flooded him. He glanced at the wastebasket, hoping he wouldn't need to vomit. "What does that have to do with me?

I've seen the freaks who've gone through the treatment. Pale, with see-through skin. Bulbous eyes. Webbed fingers. They're not human anymore. That's why we made the treatment illegal."

"I understand," Dr. Simpson said. "But it might be your best hope for a cure."

"I thought that procedure was just about trying to live longer."

"Actually no. Didn't you write the bill that banned the procedure?"

Daniel shrugged. "It was written by lobbyists for Advanced Pharma."

"Well, you must have read it."

"I skimmed it. I know the basics. It turns you into a mutant, part jellyfish, part human. It lengthens your life by doing something to your telomeres, but it changes you too, alters your body chemistry so that you're no longer human."

"Well," Dr. Simpson said, "it's a little more complicated than that. I have to admit I didn't know much about it myself until recently. Just the controversy over it. But it popped up while I was researching your condition and it's actually quite remarkable."

"It's illegal. It's an abomination."

Dr. Simpson nodded. "It's completely your decision. I respect that. But you might want to consider looking into it before you dismiss it out of hand. From what I can tell, it's the only thing that can save you. There's no guarantee it will cure you, but I can practically guarantee that conventional medicine won't save you."

"I would lose everything. They'd run me out of town. I'd have to live in one of those freak colonies on Native American reservation land, outside the jurisdiction of the United States."

"Unfortunately, that's probably true. The side effects of the treatment can't be hidden. It's too bad, in a way, that you made the procedure illegal. We can't perform it here. You would have to undergo surgery in Mexico or Belize or India."

"I won't do it."

Dr. Simpson patted his hand. "You don't have to. We'll do everything we can to manage your pain, keep you comfortable.

And of course we'll keep trying our best. There are other drug combinations we can try, but they're generally less effective than what you've been taking so far. And you're not responding well to the current treatment. Plus, as you know, surgery to remove the tumors isn't an option. The cancer has spread too rapidly. It has too many tentacles."

"I feel like you're trying to push me into compromising my principles."

"No. I'm trying to keep you alive."

"But what kind of life would it be?"

"That's for you to decide. Visit a colony. Talk to some of the people confined there. Get a sense of what their lives are like. The treatment itself, from what I've read, is not that painful. They would put you under for the first procedure, injecting the jellyfish DNA into your body. The adjustment period can last up to three weeks, during which time you will likely need further treatments as your body tries to reject the foreign material."

"I absolutely refuse to do it," Daniel said. "I'd rather die."

"That is, of course, your choice," Dr. Simpson said. "I merely want you to be an informed patient."

"Are you trying to stick it to me?"

"I don't follow."

"The Senate debate on informed patients? The ban on all trans-genetic modifications?"

"Oh," Dr. Simpson said, "was that you too? Sorry. I didn't realize."

Daniel glared at Dr. Simpson. Was the man trying to remind him of how the liberal media had skewered him for taking a stand against unnatural genetic manipulation? One thing was for sure. He wouldn't be using Dr. Simpson to perform the procedure. Then he remembered that no doctor in America could do it legally. Plus, he wouldn't do it anyway.

When he told Rebecca about his doctor visit, about the Jellyfish Treatment suggested by Dr. Simpson, he expected her to be as disgusted as he was, but she only said, "Hmm."

"You can't think I should do this," he said.

"I don't know, but it seems like traditional medicine can't save you."

"But my principles."

She smiled. "Yes, you believe in them strongly."

"I've run on a platform of integrity and conservatism. This *procedure*, this abomination, is a violation of God's natural laws."

"But if it's a matter of surviving, maybe you ought to at least do as he suggests and visit a colony."

"They wouldn't even let me inside. They know who I am, what I stand for. And if they did let me in, it would probably be so they could assault me."

"I can make some calls, see what they say."

"No. I've lived the life I wanted. I won't betray my values just to live a little longer." He felt good saying that, even though he knew deep down that it wasn't true. He wanted to live; he just didn't want to be a freak. If he could have the treatment and hide the fact that he'd done so, he'd do it in a heartbeat, principles be damned.

But he was only as good as the image he projected to the public. He was only as important as they believed he was. If he underwent the treatment and became a *thing*, he would no longer be Senator Daniel Frederick Massico IV. He'd be a slimy, pale creature deserving of vilification. How could he live with that?

Three weeks later he could no longer keep his disease a secret. Once robust, he was now little more than a caricature, a concentration camp survivor. He simply could not eat. Everything tasted terrible; nausea accompanied even the thought of food.

The media broke the story on a Friday, on a day when he felt like lying down and dying. He had almost no energy, no strength. He simply reclined in a chair in his office while Rebecca ran interference for him. Yesterday Dr. Simpson had told him the standard treatments were never going to work. He'd already tweaked the dosages as much as he could. Any more and the drugs would kill him.

"Are you sure you don't want to look at a colony?" Rebecca asked. "There's one only a few hours away."

"I may not have been as principled as I held myself out to be," he replied, "but I always aspired to be principled."

"I know," she said.

He almost couldn't remember what it was like to live without pain.

"I want you to live," she said.

"What would you think of me if I became one of those monsters?"

"I don't know," she said, wringing her hands. "This is a special case."

"Okay, we'll drive up there and take a look around. No promises."

Dr. Simpson met them at the colony entrance with another doctor, one from the colony: a woman with translucent skin—he could actually see the veins in her arms and hands and even her forehead—and bulging eyes that looked far too large to be human. Her face looked puffy, like maybe she had the DNA of a blowfish. He practically expected to see gills in her neck. Dr. Simpson introduced her as Dr. Eslinger. She extended her hand and he forced himself to shake it, trying not to notice the webbing between her fingers. He was sure he could feel it, however. Revolting.

A dozen people lined the entrance to the colony, all mutants, carrying signs that denounced him. How did they even know he was coming? When Dr. Eslinger looked away for a moment, he rubbed his hand on his slacks.

"It's going to be okay," Rebecca said.

"Jellyfish don't have eyes," he observed.

"It's called the Jellyfish Treatment," Dr. Eslinger said, "but it's not just jellyfish DNA. Even though jellyfish, from what we understand, can theoretically live forever, there are other species involved in the procedure as well."

As they walked into the colony, he detected the smell of fish and realized it came from the protesters. Clenching his jaw tightly to keep the bile down, he tried not to stare at the protesters as they chanted: "Bigot, bigot, xenophobe! Bigot, bigot, xenophobe!"

"That's enough," Dr. Eslinger said.

"He's a monster," the ugliest protester called out.

If he hadn't been in so much pain, Daniel might have smiled. He'd been thinking the exact same thing about the protester. The fish smell was almost overpowering. He noticed Rebecca wrinkling her nose, found himself doing the same.

The protesters and even Dr. Eslinger looked like aliens from some terrible late-night movie, almost comical in their near-humanness. The hands holding the signs all had webbed fingers. Like frogs. He shivered.

Dr. Eslinger led them past small, tidy houses, well cared for but all built with the same blueprint.

"How come all the houses are blue or green?" Rebecca asked.

Until that moment, Daniel hadn't noticed, but she was right. The houses were not just the same shape and size, they were all painted in variations of blue or green. Not a red house, not a white house in sight.

"We find blues and greens most soothing," Dr. Eslinger replied. It's why we only wear blue and green clothing."

Another thing he hadn't noticed. Daniel turned and stared at the protesters, still lining the entryway. Yup, all blue or green clothing.

"Doesn't anybody want a different color just to be an individual?" he asked. "Or a different size house or a different floor plan or anything?"

"We find it comforting to be part of a community."

"Like a school of fish," Dr. Simpson said.

"Exactly," Dr. Eslinger replied.

"Interesting."

"Bizarre," Daniel said. He turned to Rebecca. "Isn't it?"

She said nothing but looked pale.

"We have the same houses," Dr. Eslinger said, "because they're more affordable and many of us have difficulty getting jobs of any sort, let alone good jobs. It's not illegal to discriminate against us since, under the law, we don't have full human rights."

Thanks to me, he thought. Thanks to my efforts. No wonder they hate me. Yet they aren't human. Anyone can see that. He had just done what needed to be done. Separate out the true from the pretend people.

Dr. Eslinger showed them into her house, a cramped office making up what would presumably have been the living room. Inviting them to sit, she disappeared for a few minutes before returning with a pot of tea.

"Do you live here alone?" Daniel asked as she poured.

"My husband divorced me after I had the procedure," she answered. "He said he couldn't live with a fish."

She made the statement simply, without emotion, as if discussing a book or movie her husband hadn't liked.

"I'm sorry," Daniel said. He glanced over at Rebecca, but she was busy with her tea, avoiding his eyes. What was she thinking?

Could he ever consent to such a procedure? For now he was still human. But he could imagine himself looking like Dr. Eslinger. It nearly made him vomit to picture that in his head, but he *could* imagine it. Two days ago he wouldn't have been able to do so. What did it say about him that he could contemplate such an action? And what would Rebecca think of him if he actually did it? Would she hate him?

She seemed to want him to consider it. After all, coming here had been her idea. But now that she was here, she seemed ill at ease, distracted, upset. He realized he thought a great deal about her, about her opinion of him. He was even attracted to her. So far, however, he had avoided a physical relationship with her.

What was he thinking? Why would he even consider such a thing? He was dying. Soon. Nothing would change that unless he did the unthinkable. And he wouldn't do the unthinkable.

The rest of the meeting seemed surreal, Dr. Eslinger's words almost directed at some other person. Daniel saw how Rebecca had shut down. Only Dr. Simpson seemed to be following along, asking questions, staying engaged.

Within the hour they were done, Dr. Simpson finally recognizing that Daniel was no longer absorbing Dr. Eslinger's input. As they left, the protesters still chanting and holding up signs, painted with blue and green ink, he found himself almost unable to move. Each step cost a tremendous amount of willpower. He might have thought Dr. Eslinger put something in the tea, except that Rebecca and Dr. Simpson moved sprightly enough.

"It's a lot to take in," Dr. Simpson said. "Think it over. Perhaps you won't change your mind, but at least you'll have made a more informed decision."

Rebecca dropped him at home, walking him to his door. She opened her mouth as if intending to say something but tears began to run down her cheeks and she fled for her car, taking a moment to compose herself behind the wheel before driving away. He realized he was going to miss her. Actually, no, he wasn't. He was going to be dead. He went to bed early, sleeping poorly.

The next morning he awoke feeling as if he were having a heart attack. His chest constricted. His left arm hurting. The nanobots in his system must have sent an alert to Dr. Wells and Dr. Simpson because an ambulance arrived and took him to the hospital, where he was quickly seen and admitted. Rebecca, whom he had named as the person to notify in case of emergency, met him there. She found him reclining in bed and took a seat beside him, reaching for his hand, saying nothing.

"Just waiting for the doc," he said. "It's nothing."

She nodded, looking pale. Together they waited. But even today Rebecca seemed distracted and upset. That in turn upset him. He realized how strong his feelings for her had become. He didn't want to cause her pain. Should he tell her how he felt about her or let it go? After all, why burden her when he wouldn't be around much longer?

Dr. Simpson, after studying more nanobot data and briefly consulting with Dr. Wells, entered his room, his expression grim. "We're out of time," he said.

"What do you mean? I felt fine yesterday."

"That's the thing with this disease and with the nanobots inside you. They provide artificial boosts to your system, but in the meantime, your body is shutting down. The disease is very aggressive. The nanobots can only compensate so much, for so long, before they're overwhelmed."

"How much time do I have?"

"You'll live perhaps two more weeks unless you have the surgery now."

"What do you mean, now?"

"I mean, you have to get on a plane today and fly to Mexico. You have to undergo the Jellyfish Treatment tomorrow."

"Why so soon?"

"If you wait any longer, your body will be too weak. You wouldn't survive the procedure. I hate to sound harsh, but if you decide not to do it, that's the last choice you'll ever make. I can call a friend and get you in tomorrow if you wish. I've looked into it already just in case, but it's still your decision. I don't want to force you into anything. We can, of course, manage the pain quite nicely. We've made significant advances in hospice care, so it won't be a painful death if you decide to stay the course." He held up his phone. "Let me know if you change your mind."

After he left, Daniel caressed the back of Rebecca's hand with his thumb. "How can I do it?" he asked. "My whole life would be for nothing if I sacrificed my principles for the sake of a few more years as a freak. What would they say about me? What kind of ridicule would they heap upon me for being a flip-flopping fish?"

"Oh, Freddy," she said. "I've been such a fool."

"So have I," he said. "I should have told you long ago how I felt."

"What do you mean?"

"I'm in love with you." He felt better saying it, getting it out into the open despite the lateness of the hour, despite the fact that he wouldn't be around to act on his impulses any longer.

Rebecca's eyes opened wide. "Dear Freddy. I'm so sorry."

"Not as sorry as I am."

"No. I mean, I'm not in love with you. I love you like an uncle, but…"

"Oh." Daniel felt his face coloring with embarrassment. How could he have read her so wrongly? "Then what did you mean about being a fool?"

"My sister is in one of those colonies. She developed an autoimmune disorder that was making her life miserable. It might have killed her eventually, but it would have taken years. Decades of suffering. So she took the treatment. I haven't seen her since. But I see now how narrow-minded I was, how I shouldn't have condemned her for what she did, what she became."

"So that's why you wanted me to look into it? To reconcile with your sister?"

Rebecca shook her head. "I just didn't understand. My own sister, and I couldn't grasp why she thought it was necessary. Now I do. You made me see that."

"So what should I do?" Part of him wanted to die but mostly he wanted to live, even if it meant being a fish.

"Sometimes principles are wrong," she said. "Sometimes the things we believe in so strongly are based on ignorance. We don't know that at the time, of course, but if we're fortunate, we get the chance to figure it out. That's what I wanted to say. I've been fighting for the wrong things all this time. I finally get it. I was a fool."

"That doesn't answer my question," he said.

"No," she replied, "it doesn't. But I can't stay any longer either. I have to go see my sister. I'm sorry, Freddy. I wish you the best."

"You have to leave right now?"

She got to her feet and released his hand. "I'll be back tomorrow," she said. "And I'll stay with you until the end, for the next two weeks. I can manage that. I just can't pursue policies I no longer agree with."

"What if I changed? What if I had the procedure?"

Rebecca smiled sadly. "I know you, Freddy. You won't do it. You're so concerned about your image, your status, your legacy. You won't throw that away. You pretend it might be possible. But

I saw your face while you were there. I saw the disgust, the horror. You could never be one of them. You wouldn't last a week. You'd kill yourself."

"Maybe not," he said.

"I'll be back tomorrow," she said.

As she walked out the door, his eyes drifted to his phone on the stand beside his bed. They thought they knew him. Were they right? Would he really die for the sake of his principles? And what was so wrong with that? Better to die a human being than live as a jellyfish. Wasn't it?

He turned on the television, saw a news report about himself visiting the colony, accompanied by video of him speaking with Dr. Eslinger. The crawl on the bottom of the screen stated that he was thinking about breaking the law, having the procedure done in Mexico. How had the story gotten out so quickly? Probably one of the damn protesters. Reporters would be coming soon, jabbing their microphones in his face, demanding to know if he was the hypocrite they wanted him to be for the sake of their stories, their ratings.

No, he wasn't. He was a United States Senator, for God's sake. He would die a United States Senator.

Once again his eyes drifted to his phone. His fingers twitched.

Divination by Water

Pedro Ponce

She nestled at the pool's edge, enjoying the trickle and plash, the sensation of floating. Every few moments, water washed warmly over her shoulders and outstretched arms. She bobbed her head to a melody she remembered playing at her ear; when she attempted words to match the music, her face strained in concentration. She stopped after several tries, humming softly and watching her toenails waver like tiny corals below.

Water erupted at her side. A tall shape breached, veiled in transparent tendrils. The only discernible feature was its mouth, stubbled and open from the effort of suction. The mouth pursed around a large gulp of something. She watched air burst from the full lips. The mouth appraised her with a sliver of front teeth, weaving through dwindling ripples to join her. She watched its features coalesce, sharpen, then blur again as it erased the intervening distance, attaching itself.

* * *

She broke away, laughing. She felt a pair of thumbs slide under the top of her bathing suit.

"Not here," she admonished.

"Who's going to see?" he asked, lowering his hands to her waist. He loosened his grip so she could lean around him. She leaned as far as she could but saw nothing beyond the rippling water and the dimly lit tiles on the other side.

"Where'd everybody go?" she asked.

"There's nobody else." He looked across the blue expanse. "The water's a lot warmer out there. C'mon."

"No!"

"I'll hold you up. I promise."

"I can't—" Her words were cut off by a long yawn. She sank neck deep against the slick tiles.

* * *

"Hon?" he said.

"What?" She squinted at the distant lines scoring the bottom of the pool.

"I was just saying how nice this is. Just us."

"It hasn't been *that* long." Water dribbled into her eyes. She rubbed at the slight sting with one hand, careful to hold on to the edge with the other.

"Feels that way sometimes."

She looked in his direction. "What do you mean?"

He avoided her eyes and plunged under, rising again with a soft splash.

"What?" she repeated.

He shook his head and waded closer, gently grasping her by the hips. "I'm just glad to be here with you."

She smiled dismissively. "Whatever."

"You want to finish this?" He held up a long flute, half full of frothy liquid that smelled like coconut.

She recoiled. "Ugh. I already feel hungover."

He drained the glass in a single swallow.

* * *

"Dance with me," she said.

"Here? In front of everybody?"

She rolled her eyes and paddled awkwardly towards him, hooking her arms around his neck. She pecked at his lips. She shivered slightly as his arms braced her.

He looked down at the inlet formed by their bodies. "I've never been very good at this," he said.

"Anyone can slow dance. All you need is a partner."

They drifted, turning slowly. She hummed the melody from before. At first, it had been clear and the words muddled, but now she was having trouble remembering the music as well.

"What's that?" he asked.

"Hmm?"

"That song."

She rested her cheek against his chest and shut her eyes. "You know. We were just listening to it."

"When?"

"Just now."

"We didn't bring any music."

"No music?" she said. "It's right—" She felt herself strain at his arms. His shoulders obscured the edges of the pool.

* * *

"It's getting late," she said.

"How can you tell?"

She stifled another yawn. "What time is it?"

"I don't know," he answered.

She scanned the walls overhead. Except for the wavering light along a distant perimeter, their surroundings were dark.

"I don't think we're supposed to know."

She stared briefly. "You're being weird. I'm going to bed." She began to lift herself out.

"You can't," he said. He was behind her now, jogging her gently in place.

"Why not?" She let him hold her. Her hands swayed free in the water.

"Because we're already in bed."

Her fingers stilled. "What did you say?"

"We're already in bed. Asleep."

She puffed her lips. "You're wasted," she said. She reached a hand out of the water.

"Wait," he said, pressing his lips to her ear.

"What are you—"

"Just listen."

"Stop… you're—"

"How did we get here?"

She settled back onto his knees.

"Remember?"

She stared at the water overrunning the edge of the pool.

* * *

He began rocking her gently from side to side. "You don't remember because none of this is real."

"How can two people—"

"It happens. I saw it somewhere."

"Where?"

"On TV. One of those ghost hunting shows."

She spoke into his shoulder. "You believe that stuff?"

"I believe in keeping an open mind."

She cupped some water in her hands and watched it seep from the seam of her palms. "Two different people. In the same dream." She folded her arms and yielded to the sway of his body.

"Like they say about married people."

"We're not married," she said.

* * *

"Say it's true."

"What?"

"This is all—"

"It *is* true."

"Your arms feel real. This water feels real."

"What about this?" he asked. She yelped at the pinch of his fingers on her swimsuit. "Or this?" He pressed his lips to hers. His tongue worked at the seal of her mouth until she opened to receive him.

* * *

"Think about it. Why would we be here? Of all places."

"You wanted a glass of water. So I got out of bed. When I came back, you were out cold."

"Then what?"

"Then I watched you sleep. I like watching you sleep. It's like I'm protecting you."

She nestled back against the edge and poked her toes out of the water. "From what?"

"That movie star you're always mumbling about."

She slapped the surface, splashing him.

* * *

"How do we wake up?"

"Don't you like it here?"

She leaned into him. "My dreams are never this quiet."

"Maybe it's a nightmare," he whispered into her shoulder.

"Don't."

"Like one of those shows. *When Sharks Go Apeshit*." He sank his teeth into her shoulder.

"Ow!"

"Sorry."

She pulled away. "I'm getting out."

"Hon—"

"I want to wake up. Right now."

"Take it easy."

"Help me wake up. Help me—"

"It doesn't work like that."

"How do you know?"

He let himself drift away towards the center of the pool.

"Where are you going?" she asked.

"You figure it out."

She turned and studied her fingers. "Okay," she yelled over her shoulder. "I will." She propped herself up using the edge for support. Her arms shook from the effort and the cold on her wet skin. She sank back, shivering.

* * *

"We were fighting."

"What?"

"We were fighting. Before."

He dove under and emerged inches from her perch.

"I didn't want to—So you got out of bed." She slid towards him. "You were gone a long time."

"I needed to—"

"That's not what I mean. I heard you open the medicine cabinet." She slapped the water hard, sending spray into the air. "What were you doing in the medicine cabinet?"

He shook himself off. "How could you even—"

"I've only asked you to oil the fucking door every day for the last month."

He immersed himself up to his chin. "I had a headache. I took something."

"I don't believe you."

"That was *your* excuse."

* * *

He floated towards her, making a show of how careful he was being, paddling slowly so that only his head appeared above water. Despite this, his approach caused icy wavelets to rise above the straps of her bathing suit. She turned away and shivered into her folded arms.

"Hey," he said. He drifted behind her, lacing his fingers through hers. He picked a strand of hair clinging to her cheek and placed it carefully behind her ear. She let him hold her.

"Don't you see how amazing this is? Our own little world. Nobody else."

"It doesn't make any sense."

He let go abruptly and treaded water in front of her.

"What are you doing?"

"Close your eyes."

"They're already closed."

"Good. Keep them that way."

She heard nothing beyond the slap of water against tiles.

"Just wait," he said. "I need to concentrate."

"What for?"

"I'm taking us somewhere else. Somewhere better. Watch. No—wait. Eyes closed."

She heard a light splash nearby. "Where'd you go?" she asked. "Where are you?"

* * *

"You did something."

"What did I do now?"

"To me."

"You think—"

She released the edge and flailed towards him. When she reached him, she grasped his waist and clambered up.

"I was mad," she said. "But—" Her mouth twisted indecipherably.

He raised her by the arms and propped her head on his shoulders. He stroked her back gently as it convulsed.

"You didn't have to—" she managed to whisper. "I say lots of things when I'm mad. We both do."

He swayed her from side to side until the coughing stopped. "You scared me."

"I'm sorry."

"You shouldn't scare me like that."

She had regained her breath but the tightness of his grip made her breathing shallow. She could feel the shake of his shoulders at her chin. "Honey? Are you—"

"You shouldn't scare me like that," he repeated.

* * *

A grinning mass appeared, pink transparent plastic. Its thick tail, ridged like a dinosaur's, angled diagonally above the water. Its neck was long and reticulated like a worm. The bulbous head was triangular, like its teeth, which were scrawled in an off-white patchwork along one side. The nostrils reminded her of a flaring horse's, while its eyes stared blankly at her, through the luster of beading water. Slowly, the float turned, revealing drooped wings that cleaved the water's surface. The neck, limbs, and tail were joined by a square base, with a hollow at the center the size of a child's torso. Water burbled along the sides of the hollow as the float completed its turn.

* * *

"I never dream about water," she said.

"Nobody remembers all their dreams."

"I remember enough." She spun around.

"This is different."

She slid herself over until she was directly in front of him. "You never answered me. What did you give me?"

"I swear—"

"We're not supposed to wake up. We're not supposed to… This isn't—"

She tried to dodge his approach, but his arms were too quick. He linked his hands tightly over her belly and pulled her towards him.

"What did you do?"

"I needed to show you."

"Show me what?"

He traced her earlobe with the tip of his nose. "Where you go, I go."

* * *

"I'm cold," she said.

He gripped her more tightly against him.

"I want to leave."

He kissed the line of her jaw. "We are."

"Tell me again."

"Tell you—"

"Tell me again."

He turned her around and held her head with both hands. "You have to trust me."

"I want... I want to leave."

"Then you know what we have to do."

She sobbed, pressing her eyes against his splayed thumbs. "Why?"

"Because it's the only way. Hey," he said, shaking her.

"I never—"

"Hey." He shook her more forcefully.

"Let go."

"Are you going to stop crying?"

She looked at him. His hands drifted to her sides.

* * *

"Ready?" he asked.

She nodded and settled herself next to him. She pressed her feet to the tiles. She looked for her ankles in the churn of sudden current. She bent with him as he leaned back.

"Will you make me breakfast?" she asked.

His grip on her slackened. "What?"

"In the morning. Will you make me breakfast?"

"Sure." She could see his teeth in the periphery of her vision. She readied herself, knees just breaching the surface.

"I'm not cold anymore."

"No?"

"The water feels soft. Like—"

"Blankets?"

She nodded. "Blankets. And blue. It's like—" Her breath caught. The water was up to her chin now.

"Don't," he said. He gripped her shoulder.

They leaned once more towards the tiles, which reflected them back in concentric streaks. Together they pushed off.

Graceland

Rick Polad

I had wrapped up two cases over the weekend and was looking forward to making the six-hour drive to Door County, Wisconsin, to escape the Chicago summer heat. Thoughts of a week sitting on the deck of my cabin on Moonlight Bay were enticing. I finished my notes on the Shackley case and was about to walk them in to Carol when the front door opened, letting in the noise of the car traffic on Fullerton. I sat back down and hoped it was the mailman. It wasn't. I heard enough to know it was a male and then heard Carol say, "He's in… one moment."

She timidly peeked into my office with an apologetic look. "Spencer, there's a—"

I cut her off with a wave and a shake of my head. "Send him in."

He was a large man who looked to be in pretty good shape for someone I guessed was in his eighties. But there was something odd about him that I couldn't put my finger on. He seemed to move without effort as he sat in the wooden chair in front of my desk.

I stood and held out my hand. "Good morning, I'm Spencer Manning."

He didn't offer his hand, but nodded, smiled, and said, "I'm Gary Owens. Thank you for seeing me."

I sat, asked how I could help him, and tried not to take it personally that he didn't want to shake my hand.

"Well, it's a bit worrisome, you know. I have a granddaughter who means everything to me. And if I may say, I mean everything to her. Her name is Patricia… she's the most wonderful person you'd ever want to meet."

"And Patricia is in trouble?"

"Well, now she may be… and then again she may not be."

I waited but he was done talking. And I was getting frustrated. "What is it you want, Mr. Owens?"

"I'd like you to find out."

"Find out what?"

"If she is or isn't."

I just knew Carol was trying not to laugh.

"What kind of trouble might she be in?"

"*That* I'm not sure of, but she's had a tough time of it the last four years and I'm afraid she's fallen in with the wrong sort."

"And what is it you want me to do?"

"Just have a chat with her and set her straight."

He seemed like a sweet old man but there was something not right. He was confused. "Have *you* had a chat with her, Mr. Owens?"

"Well, I'd like to… I certainly would, but I can't quite manage it at the moment."

A part of me wanted to ask why, but a bigger part of me wanted to get in my baby-blue Mustang and head north. "I'd like to help you, but having chats isn't something I do. This is a detective agency, not a counseling service."

His face lit up with a big smile. "That's it exactly! I want you to do some detecting."

I'm sure I wasn't hiding my confusion. "You said you wanted me to have a chat with her."

"Oh, I do, sir! But first you have to find her."

I didn't have to wonder about Carol… I heard the laugh.

He seemed like one of those old people Dad told me about who called the police with some complaint just to have someone to talk to. I felt sorry for him, but if I could leave in an hour I'd be putting a steak on the grill for dinner.

"I'm sorry, Mr. Owens, but I have several cases I'm working on and I just don't have time at the moment."

His smile disappeared, replaced by a look of utter sadness.

"I *had* hoped you could help, sir. She means everything to me."

I gave up on my steak and asked, "When was the last time you talked to her?"

Now he looked confused. "Well, it's been four years, but I've been keeping tabs on her. I know she misses me."

I had no idea how to help this sad old man. I was even wondering if he *had* a granddaughter. But he looked so distraught I wanted to do something.

"Can you tell me her address?"

"Yes, but that won't help... she's not there. She's missing, you see."

"I still need an address if I'm going to look."

He nodded and looked puzzled. "Well, you could try 2418 Addison. She has an apartment there."

"Okay. Good. Have you called the police?"

"Oh, no, sir. I cannot do that."

The front door opened again. This time it *was* the mailman.

I was hopeful about the steak. "Missing persons is best handled by the police, Mr. Owens. I have friends on the force who would handle this personally. I'll even make the call right now while you're here so you can talk to them."

He stood, shaking his head. "No, sir, that won't do. You were recommended. If you won't look, I'm afraid all hope is lost."

I sighed and asked him to sit. "Okay, I'll check at her apartment, but if I don't find anything there, I'm afraid that's all I can do. The police really are better equipped to find someone."

He slowly shook his head.

I sighed. "How old is she?"

"Just twenty-one."

"Okay. Leave your contact information with my secretary. She'll fill you in on my fees and have you sign an agreement."

He bowed his head, stared at his lap, and very quietly said, "I'm afraid I can't pay you."

This kept getting better, but now I was hooked and wondering what the hell was going on. If nothing else, I could bring some relief to this confused old man. And most of my cases were charity anyway. I had a trust fund my folks left me and had the luxury of being able to choose the cases I took. Most were people who needed help but couldn't pay, or couldn't pay much. When I did get a paying customer I donated it to the police fund.

"Okay then, Mr. Owens. Do you have a picture of Patricia?"

He sadly shook his head. "Not with me, I don't."

"Then give me a description."

He did. Long blond hair, a little over five feet, thin, and the most beautiful woman God ever made.

"Okay, then just leave your phone number and address with Carol. I'll check out her apartment this afternoon and get back to you."

"Bless you, sir. I'll do that."

I waited until I heard the door open and close and then walked into the front reception area. Carol handed me a slip of paper with Mr. Owens' address and the address of his granddaughter.

"He didn't give you a phone number?"

"Says he doesn't have one. He doesn't like these newfangled machines."

I had to agree with him there. A friend who works for Motorola had just given me a gadget he called a portable cell phone he said they were bringing out soon. But the damned thing was as big as a shoebox—not very portable.

"I'm glad you agreed to look into it, Spencer. I feel sorry for him."

"This doesn't make much sense."

"No, he's just confused. But he does seem to love his granddaughter."

I agreed. "If he *has* a granddaughter. I'm betting the apartment building on Addison doesn't exist."

"Then you can at least tell him you tried."

* * *

It did exist and it did have the name tag of 'Patricia Owens' on one of nine mailboxes in the foyer. I rang the bell under the mailbox and waited ten seconds before I rang again. No answer. I rang the bell of the manager—the tag said 'Barry.' A woman answered. She let me in after I told her I was looking for Patricia. She buzzed the door and was waiting for me at the first apartment. I gave her my card and introduced myself.

She looked at it and me carefully and invited me in. We sat at her metal kitchen table.

"So, why are you looking for Patricia?"

I didn't want to mention her grandfather. I still wasn't sure about him. "There is some concern about her welfare. Have you seen her recently, Mrs. Barry?"

"Come to think of it, I haven't seen her in a few weeks... not that I see all my tenants, but Patricia would stop and chat if I was working in the garden. A nice girl."

"Would it be possible to have a look in her apartment?"

She looked around the room like she had to check with someone, but there was no one else there. "That's unusual, but since I haven't seen her... Do you think she's dead in the apartment?"

"I don't think anything at the moment. But let's check."

She shook her head vehemently. "Because I certainly don't want someone dying in my apartments. That's just not good publicity."

"It wouldn't be good for Patricia either."

"I suppose not."

I followed her to the third floor where she opened the door to 3B and tentatively walked in. It was a small apartment with a living room, one bedroom, a bath, and a kitchen. It needed some serious remodeling. Nothing looked out of place in the living room.

Nothing looked out of place in the rest of the rooms either. But there was a picture of Patricia and her grandfather on the dresser. I slipped it out of the frame and into my pocket.

I thanked Mrs. Barry for her help. She looked relieved. Her reputation was safe.

"Can you tell me anything about her?"

"Like what?"

"Friends? Do you know where she worked or hung out?"

She shrugged. "She didn't have any friends here. These are mostly older people. And I don't think she worked. But I can tell you she paid her rent on time every month."

I wondered how that could be. "Anything else?"

"Well, I don't know if I should say... I don't like to speak ill of anyone."

As long as they didn't die in her apartments, I thought. "She may be missing, Mrs. Barry. Anything you can tell me might help."

She looked around again. There still wasn't anyone there.

"Okay. One of the men here said he has seen her in the bar down the street... and with some pretty seedy looking characters. I don't even think she's twenty-one."

"Do you know the name?"

"Only because I pass it on the way to the grocery. It's the Brown Tap."

I thanked her and, not wanting to lose my parking space, walked to the Brown Tap. Walking that block worked up a sweat.

* * *

It was a typical neighborhood bar that had just opened for lunch. I was the only customer. The bartender greeted me warmly as I sat at the bar. He asked what my pleasure was. I told him I was just looking for information but, as long as it was lunchtime and I was hungry, I'd have a pastrami on rye and a Schlitz.

He brought the beer and we chatted while I waited for my sandwich. I showed him Patricia's picture and asked if he recognized her.

He did. She had been coming in almost every night, but he hadn't seen her for a while.

"She have any friends she hung out with?"

He was still looking at the picture as he slowly said, "Yeah, there was one guy. Big fellow... older than her."

"Do you have a name?"

"Just a first. Ian. English accent. Pretty good with a pool cue."

"How much older?"

"Around thirty."

"Have you seen him recently?"

"He's here every night… except Sunday. We close at six."

"If I come back tonight, could you point him out to me?"

"Well, I leave at six today, but you can't miss him what with the accent and all. He draws a crowd. Usually shows up around ten."

I thanked him and thought about the case while I ate my sandwich and finished the beer. My thoughts weren't getting me very far. But at least my method of shaking the trees and seeing what fell out had led me to the next step. Dreading leaving the air conditioning, I savored the pastrami and the beer.

* * *

I stopped back at the office, filled Carol in, and called Lt. Powolski. My dad had been chief of police until he and Mom were killed in a car accident three years ago. I had grown up with the lieutenant, 'Uncle Stosh,' who was as much a member of the family as I was. Saturday afternoons were now reserved for gin rummy and watching the Cubs with him.

I filled him in on the case and asked if someone could check on Patricia and her grandfather. I gave him all the information I had. He made his usual comment about the department not being on my payroll and hung up.

I headed home and used the excuse of not knowing how late I would be up to get in a nap. Any excuse would do.

* * *

I got back to the Brown Tap a little after nine and nursed another Schlitz at the bar. At five to ten I heard the English accent greeting the crowd at the pool table. I found Ian in the mirror above the bar. I didn't see Patricia. My plan was to follow him home and confront him there without his army of buddies. He closed the place at one.

My Mustang was two blocks away and I had no idea if he had a car. If he did I'd get the plate number and make another call to Stosh. He didn't. He headed north from the bar and went into a house in the third block.

I watched as the lights went on but I didn't see anyone else in the house. The kitchen light went off and I expected to see the lights come on upstairs. Instead, a light showed in the window well of the basement. That went off five minutes later and then the light came on upstairs. Ten minutes after that the house was dark. I walked up and down the block for another half hour and the house stayed dark.

As I walked past for the last time a car pulled out from a spot two houses to the south. My plan was to come back in the morning and wait for Ian to leave. I needed to get in the house. But, seeing as how I had just been handed a parking space, I decided to spend the night. On the way back to my car, I walked up the block and down the alley. There was no garage and the property was surrounded by a high fence just a little shorter than my six-feet-two. The back yard was full of weeds and a back door was in the middle of a dilapidated deck.

The parking spot was still there when I got back, and a breeze off the lake had cooled the evening down to the point where I could spend the night in the car and not be totally miserable.

I slept pretty well for being scrunched behind a steering wheel. I was used to spending nights in that position but I was always awake on a stakeout. I was awakened by the sound of a slamming car door at 5:42. I yawned and got out to stretch my legs. I kept close enough to watch the house and an hour later got back in the car. Ian appeared at 7:05. I sat in the Mustang listening to WGN until ten when I figured everyone going to work had already left. I took my lock picks out of the glove compartment and hopped the fence in the alley.

The back door was no problem. It took me ten seconds to get inside. I watched out the window into the backyard for ten minutes and saw nothing and no one. It took fifteen minutes to walk through the first and second floors. The place was a mess, but I found nothing out of the ordinary. I saved the basement for last.

I took a towel from the kitchen and turned the knob on what I thought was the basement door. It didn't turn. Who would lock their basement door? That lock was actually harder to pick than the back door, but a minute later I had it opened. I flipped the switch just inside the door and started down.

One dim, bare bulb cast a ghostly yellow glow over a cluttered room with a furnace in one corner and walls lined with shelves and benches covered with tools. Typical basement. There was nothing strange, but there was another door on the street-side wall. It was locked, but this one was easier. I felt for a light switch but didn't find one. The only light was coming from the bare bulb by the furnace. I stepped into the room and let my eyes adapt to the dim light. The room was empty except for a toilet in one corner and a bed against the outside wall. And there was someone on the bed covered with a sheet.

I said hello and got no response. I pulled back a corner of the sheet and found Patricia. I couldn't tell if she was breathing so I felt her neck and found a weak pulse. But I couldn't rouse her.

Thinking that the shoebox phone would have come in handy, I went upstairs and called Stosh. Ten minutes later, a fire department ambulance and two police cars pulled up in front. Detective Rosie Lonnigan and her partner Mike Kelley followed the medics up the front stoop.

"How does trouble keep finding you, Spencer?" she asked.

"Kinda comes with the job, Rosie. You found me, didn't you?"

"We all have our crosses to bear," she said with a smile.

I led them all to the basement. The medics said Patricia appeared to be drugged but wasn't in any danger. That had been my guess. We all followed the ambulance to the hospital.

* * *

By three p.m. Patricia was awake enough to talk. She was giving a statement to Rosie when I walked into the room. She had been hanging around the bar for months and had made friends with Ian. About two weeks ago, he had convinced her to come home with him. She remembered struggling as he put a rag over her mouth. She vaguely remembered lying on a bed in a room with a toilet in the corner. She asked Rosie how they found her. Rosie introduced me.

"Well, then I have you to thank, Mr. Manning. But how did you know to look for me?"

"You can thank your grandfather for that."

She looked confused, but I knew she hadn't fully recovered from the drugs.

"My grandfather? I don't know what you mean. Who hired you?"

"Well, your grandfather."

She started to cry and tremble.

"Thank you for finding me, Mr. Manning, but you don't have to be mean."

Now *I* was confused. "Mean? What are you talking about? When you're up to it I'll take you to him."

"Get out!" she screamed through tears. "You're the meanest person I've ever met!"

"I don't—"

"Get out! Get out!"

I tried to respond, but Rosie took my arm and led me out of the room.

As the door closed, I said, "What the hell was that about, Rosie?"

"Let's go to the waiting room. I think I can explain."

We sat in a quiet corner with me still wondering what had just happened.

"You can explain that?"

"Well, sort of."

"Sort of?"

She took a deep breath. "As I was walking into the hospital I got a call from Stosh. We ran your Gary Owens. The address he gave you was 4001 N. Clark?"

"Best as I remember."

She sighed. "That's Graceland cemetery."

"Oh great, he gave me a bogus address."

"Well, sort of."

"Rosie! Stop with the sort ofs!"

"Sorry, Spencer, that's the best I can do."

"What the hell does that mean?"

Another deep breath. "That's his address, but it's not all of his address."

"Good. That clears it up."

"Maybe this will. It's 4001 N. Clark, plot 1307."

I stared at her for what seemed like an hour, but it was only a minute. "What does that mean? Is he living in one of the crypts?"

She shook her head. "No, he's buried there.

I stared some more.

"Spencer, Gary Owens died four years ago."

"Rosie, he was in my office. He was worried about his granddaughter."

"And he had reason to be."

"You're saying the person sitting in my chair was... wasn't... a person?"

She shrugged. "I'm not saying anything. I'm just telling you the facts. You're the big PI. You figure it out."

"You're saying that the Gary Owens in my office was a... a... spirit?"

"Again, Spencer, I have no answers. I just have a girl who is safe and you have another successful case. But this time maybe you had a little help."

"Help how?"

"Not how... who."

"Okay, I'll bite... who?"

"Well, let's say Gary Owens, deceased for four years, walks into a heavenly bar and sits down with Chief of Police Manning.

The conversation turns to his worry about his granddaughter, and your dad says he knows just the guy to help."

"You can't be serious."

"You have a better answer, let me hear it. That's mine."

I told her I'd pick her up at five at the station. She was buying dinner... and beer... lots of beer.

Sara

Carolyn Killion

"Don't anticipate, wait." He swung his sword around and the crack of his blow sent her smaller sword flying out of her hand.

"Damn it," she muttered as she stared at it. In the backdrop of the sun, his slightly longer red hair was a blazing halo around his head. She snorted.

"Don't curse," he said. His face was too dark to see given the sun's intensity, but she imagined a scowl accompanied his words. It usually did.

"Stop telling me what to do."

He ignored her and walked the few steps to her sword. Arching her shoulders into a stretch, she held it for a moment before dropping to the ground to sit cross-legged. He set both swords next to his Jeep while she reclined on her back, feeling the cool grass through the light cotton of her black Iron Maiden T-shirt. Stretching her arms out, she looked up into the cloudless blue sky. A light breeze blew a few wisps of long brown hair across her cheek and nose.

She felt the brush of his head as he lay opposite her, the crown of his head barely touching hers.

"Why do you continue to waste your time with me, Barac?" she asked. His full name was Barachiel. She'd shortened it to a more pleasant nickname. At least he'd stopped wincing when she used it.

He didn't respond right away. He did this often, would wait the span of a few breaths before speaking. Almost every time he visited she had questions. Sometimes he answered, sometimes he didn't. It drove her nuts, which might be part of his plan.

"You have your mom in you," he said.

"That's it? That's your answer?" She shifted her head to knock his.

"Yes." He moved his head to the side to avoid hers.

"That's baloney," she said.

"Keep practicing," he told her and pushed to his feet. She looked up at him, but his face was still obscured by the sun.

"Maybe," she responded and closed her eyes. A few moments later she heard his Jeep start up, then pull away. She huffed. The man could appear and disappear at will, yet he drove a Jeep.

Lying there for a few more moments, she enjoyed the feel of the sun. Lifting her arms to the sky, she wiggled her fingers in the soft breeze. Other than getting dinner at some point, she had no plans for the day. Sushi sounded good. There was a place not too far from her townhouse that offered decent takeout.

She rolled over, pushed to her knees and slowly stood. That's what she'd do. She'd head home, pick up food to go, curl up and read a book. Her bookshelf was full of partially unread books and tonight would be a perfect time to finish one.

Sara pulled keys out of her pocket and unlocked her white Honda Accord. Her dad had frowned at her conservative choice of a reliable, economical vehicle. He'd tried to gift her a sleek black Lamborghini Veneno, but she'd donated it to the local homeless shelter the next day. She liked her Honda.

It wasn't the first time she'd disappointed her father. He'd had such big plans for her. Her mother had been ashamed of the liaison that produced her. Regardless of the circumstances of her birth, Sara had enjoyed a happy childhood. She'd been raised by a wonderful, well-to-do foster family, with intermittent visits from her father and his extended family. Her mother had never wanted anything to do with her. Sara strove each day to strike a balance between the two extremes she descended from and live a simple, uncomplicated life. It wasn't easy. But, she reasoned, life wasn't easy for anyone.

Barachiel never met her close to her house, but always in a location at least a few hours away. She started her car and pulled out of the gravel parking lot, heading home. The visits were never pre-planned. He never gave her advance warning, only sent a text with GPS coordinates when he wanted to meet. It riled her that he sent coordinates, but not an address. Each training session started with a driving adventure.

Rolling down the windows, she stuck her arm out and waved it in the breeze. She wasn't quite sure where she was, not knowing the surrounding area very well. She'd gone past a few rolling hills and came to a flat plain that spread for miles until it dipped into the horizon. Up ahead, a gas station sat next to a few dilapidated old houses. The houses were of similar size and shape, wood-sided cookie cutter types from the fifties, and each had peeling white paint. The gas station looked to be open as the lights over the gas pumps were on and a little blue sedan was parked next to one of the pumps.

Drawing closer, she decided it would be a good idea to top off her tank and maybe grab a bottle of water or apple juice. Even though she hadn't seen traffic for miles, she put on her right blinker and pulled into the station. She parked, turned her car off, grabbed her wallet and stepped out. The cool air hit her arms and raised the hairs. Reaching into the backseat, she grabbed a light pink sweater and pulled it over her head.

A glance at the pump showed that it was old and not set up for credit cards. She'd have to pay in person. When she did, she'd grab something to drink. She looked over to the other vehicle. No one was near the blue car. They must have gone inside to pay.

Inside the store, she grabbed an orange juice, instead of the apple juice she wanted. They only had orange, but it was better than the lukewarm water in the broken cooler section.

At the counter, a young man with a blue shirt and ball cap stood waiting for her. He was the only other person she could see. She set the orange juice on the counter and opened her wallet. She heard a loud crack and for a few brief seconds wondered if the ceiling had fallen on her. Then blackness engulfed her.

Some time later, she awoke with a throbbing on the side of her head. From the dull ache, she guessed someone had knocked her out. Growing up, during visits to her dad, she'd scrapped and tumbled with enough cousins on his side of the family to know what a good whack upside the head felt like.

In her somewhat disoriented state, Sara tried to sit up and found that her hands had been bound behind her. Great, not only had someone knocked her out, but they had decided to tie her up to make it an extra special experience. She twisted and used her elbow to push herself into a sitting position. At least the jerks that had done this had left her legs unbound. She stretched and looked around.

"Fuck, fuck, fuck, fuck, fuck!" she mumbled in rapid succession. There went her sushi. The place was only open until eight on Sunday nights and the darkened skies out the dingy window to her left informed her that her plans for dinner would need to be changed.

"Ah, sleeping beauty's awake." A figure approached her from the other side of the dim room. It looked like an attic, with a few high windows and open rafters. One unfinished pine chair, the type you'd buy and assemble from a big box store, stood in the middle of the room.

The man moving toward her had on blue jeans and a button-up blue and red plaid shirt. She looked down at his tan construction boots, wondering briefly if they had steel toes and why they were so new before looking up at his face. His features showed a simple, patrician nose, close-cropped dark brown hair and a smattering of whiskers. His face badly needed a shave.

Yet it was his eyes that had her dropping her head. They were flat black. No pupils, no whites, no color. All black. She let her chin rest on her collarbone for a moment. Every cuss word she'd ever heard ran through her mind, and there were a lot of them.

She lifted her head back up to look at him. She could see that he was hoping to surprise her. Unfortunately, she was going to disappoint him.

"I'm not sleeping and I'm not a beauty," she told him.

He stopped at her feet and sneered at her. His body stiffened. Her insolence and lack of fear had riled him up. She lifted the corners of her mouth in defiance.

The door on the opposite side of the room opened and the clerk from the gas station stepped in, pulling a woman behind him. She clawed at his hand but he ignored her attempts to free herself and dragged her forward by her long blond ponytail. In his other hand, he grasped the collar of a light gray jacket, under which resided a small towheaded boy of about four.

"Look what else I found hiding in the bathroom downstairs," the second man told the first. Cancel that. They weren't men. Their obsidian eyes identified them as demons.

"Awesome," the second one chuckled. He grabbed the child by the shoulders and flung him in the air. The little boy shrieked and wildly grabbed for the demon, who laughed again, a sinister sound.

Revulsion rolled through Sara's stomach. She twisted her wrists, attempting to free herself from her bonds. She had been tied with a heavy rope.

The second demon shoved the woman hard against the wall. She slammed into it and collapsed onto the scarred, old wooden floor. The other demon continued to toss the child up, laughing as the boy shrieked in terror.

"Play with her first?" the demon closest to the woman asked the other one. He grinned and continued to stare at the woman curled on the floor, crying. His light blue T-shirt displayed the gas station's logo on the front and he wore blue jeans with nondescript gray tennis shoes. His eyes were as black as the other demon's, and his hair was hidden under a dark blue gas station ball cap. Sara hadn't gotten a chance to look in his eyes before the blow to her head.

The other demon, the taller of the two and the one tossing the child, grabbed the child mid-air and tossed him onto the floor next to the mother. The little boy fell with a thud and army-crawled toward his mom, trying to get closer to the safety she represented.

Sara looked up and glanced at two forms that emerged above the mother and child. Two pale figures shimmered and solidified, folded their hands in front of them, bowed their heads and began praying.

"Are you kidding me? You're going to pray?" she whispered at them. They ignored her and continued their prayer.

The taller demon heard her and approached. He knelt down and smirked at her.

"Oh, you see angels, do you?" he said and rocked on his heels. A slow, deliberate back and forth, back and forth, his black eyes never leaving her.

Sara stared back at him. He was taunting her. Her silence taunted him back.

He curled his lip back in a sneer, reached forward and slapped her. Her head snapped to the side. She still didn't answer.

"Well, if you want to play it that way," he said and slapped her face in the opposite direction. Her head thudded against the wall and banged down against her chest. Now both sides of her head were throbbing.

"Let me go," she growled from between clenched teeth.

He set his arms on his bent knees, tossed back his head and laughed.

Anger made her cheeks hot. She kicked out and caught him under the chin with the sole of a floral-patterned Doc Marten. His head snapped back with a crack and, unbalanced, he fell over backwards.

"Let me go, then let's you and me have a little talk." She kept her voice low.

He snarled at her and jumped to his feet. Pulling his leg back, he kicked her in the stomach. Hard. Pain blossomed and she fell on her side, gasping as the breath was forced from her lungs. Several more kicks, and tears began to leak from her eyes.

"I'll let you go when it's your turn," he said. She heard heavy footsteps as he walked back over to the crying woman and the other demon.

"Let me go and let's have a little talk," he mimicked her. "Yeah, I'll talk to you in a minute."

"The idiot doesn't even notice I don't have an angel next to me," she whispered to herself and laughed a little.

She drew in a few shaky breaths and opened her eyes in time to see both demons pull knives and simultaneously stab the woman in the chest. The woman and Sara both screamed at the same time, heightening the demons' pleasure. They laughed and stabbed again. Blood stained the knives and the woman's long-sleeved shirt.

Tears streamed down the child's cheeks. He had drawn his knees up to his chest and was rocking.

"Do something," Sara told the guardian angels standing above the woman and child, praying. The angels opened their eyes and looked at her.

"We cannot interfere," the one closer to her said.

"Yes, you can!" Sara yelled.

"Can, but won't!" the taller demon jeered and pointed the bloody knife at the angels. "Can, but won't!" he repeated and laughed as he stabbed the woman again.

"We are only supposed to encourage and look over our charges, not interfere," the other angel told her. Her eyes were sad. She looked down at the woman and began another round of silent praying.

"Then call another angel!" Sara cried, "Damn it, do something!" The angels ignored her and kept praying.

"Listen, bitch, shut up or you're next, before the kid." The smaller demon pointed his bloody knife at her.

It wasn't the name-calling that sent her over the edge. It was the blatant disregard for life and the angels standing by, passive. Furious, she decided she'd had enough. She clenched her fists and tore her hands apart. The ropes snapped and she shook the remains from her wrists as she hopped to her feet.

The tall one in the plaid shirt bent over and stuck the knife through the woman's side with another malevolent snicker. The demons had not yet seen that Sara was free as they continued to plunge their knives into the woman. There was no more screaming. The blond woman's eyes were closed now and her body still.

Sara sucked in a breath and reached upward, calling to the sword on the celestial plane. There was a tugging in her middle, enhancing the pain she already felt. She closed her eyes, willing it to go away and pulled harder, to the place just out of reach. The one that the archangel Barachiel had taught her existed and how to access. He'd been training her and while she'd had no intention of ever doing anything with the training, she had a tough time standing by while two humans were gleefully murdered in front of her.

Another sucking sound came from the corner, another snicker of evil joy and a helpless boy's responding whimper to his mother being stabbed. Sara looked over in time to see the smaller demon pull his knife across the woman's throat and then push her body forward into an abandoned heap. To them, she was now as worthless as trash. The angel standing closest to the woman disappeared.

Sara screamed and pulled harder. Both demons turned as a sword of silver appeared in her hand. Their eyes widened and shock rippled across their features. The remaining angel stopped praying and looked up, her surprise matching the demons'.

A celestial sword had the ability to end the demons' lives. They wouldn't be sent back to hell, but would instead cease to exist. Very few things were able to kill demons, but a celestial sword was one of them. Sara grasped the sword with both hands and took a step forward.

The tall one lifted his knife at her. The smaller of the two wasn't as sure as his murderous partner. He glanced at the sword and at his own knife, then back at her sword. He took a step back.

"Yeah, that's what I thought," Sara hollered and lunged at him. The tall one thrust at her and she swung the sword, but he jumped back in time, missing the blade. Sara sliced again and the demon retreated again. Another swipe and she had his back to the wall. Even though it was only a few strokes, the pain in her side and head had her breathing hard. She glared at him and glanced toward the other demon, making sure he stayed put.

The black eyes of the demon trapped against the wall looked at her, as she stared at him. Her shoulders dropped a little, and she felt defeated even though she had the upper hand. She realized she had a problem. If she killed them with a celestial sword, that would involve her in their matters and she needed to remain neutral or all Hell would break loose.

She stepped back, releasing the demon. She took a few more steps away from the demons and the boy. Her body was shaking in anger and denial but she couldn't end the demons. Instead, she began to speak words so ancient that no human had a history of them.

"Are you fucking crazy? Do you want to destroy us all?" the demon shouted at her.

Sara stopped her incantation and stared at the demon, her mouth slack at his question. She raised an eyebrow.

"Oh, destroy us all?" She gestured at the bloody carcass of the woman lying at the demons' feet. "Really?" She tossed up her hands and the tip of her sword bounced against the rafter above her. She ducked her head. She didn't need another whack to the noggin, not even a self-inflicted one.

"This was just a bit of fun. What you are doing is insane," the demon said.

Sara dropped her hands to her side and resumed chanting. The demons backed away from her as her words became louder and stronger. A strong wind whipped around the room, tugging at her hair and picking up bits of dust and lint.

A menacing growl filled the room and a black shadow formed in the middle, crushing the chair. Splintered pieces of wood flew in different directions as a huge, dark red demon took shape. He filled the center of the room, standing over seven feet tall. Large, thick horns curved up from his temples and his massive frame was slick with sweat from the heat he exuded. His midsection and arms were dense cords of muscles and his lower half was covered in a black pair of sweatpants. Shiny black forked hooves clicked on the wooden floor.

Beelzebub, Prince of Hell, stood in the center, glowering and angry to have been called from the depths of the underworld.

"Who dares summon me?" the massive demon demanded, as his eyes swept across the demons, angels and humans.

Uncle Bub!" Sara squealed and ran at him. She dropped the sword as she leapt into the air. The huge demon opened his arms and caught her in a tight bear hug.

"My little Sara!" The demon tightened his embrace and twirled her around. He squeezed her one more time before setting her back on her feet.

Sara stood back and smiled at him. "I've missed you," she said.

"I've missed you too," he responded, but didn't return her smile. He took another quick glance around the room. Catching sight of the abandoned sword, he frowned. He returned his gaze to her and raised his eyebrows.

"Now, sweetie, how did you learn to pull a celestial sword?" he asked.

"Oh, Barachiel's been teaching me." She shrugged and continued to smile at him. With a flick of her wrist, she waved the sword away. It vanished, leaving no trace.

"Honeybear, in the history of humans, Barachiel has never come down out of the heavens for something so mundane." Beelzebub's eyes darkened a shade blacker than the bottomless obsidian they already were.

"Oh, he doesn't come only for a little visit and chat. He's here to ensure I'm playing ball for the celestial side." She wiggled her eyebrows up and down.

Beelzebub tossed his head back and a deep, throaty laughed erupted.

"Oh, little Sara bean, I do love you." He grabbed and bear-hugged her again. She squeezed him back. She missed the big demon's hugs. They always had the power to soothe her soul and lift her spirits when she was feeling low.

The soft whimpering of the child brought Sara back to the matter at hand. She peered around Uncle Bub's massive shoulder at the demons standing near the slain woman and weeping child.

They were staring at her, mouths agape, their hands limp at their sides, knives held loose and forgotten. She pushed out of her uncle's meaty arms.

"Now, you little fuckers, let's talk," she snapped at the cowering demons. "Meet Uncle Bub."

"Uncle Bub, meet a few little pansy-assed demon motherfuckers," she said and pointed at them.

"You didn't introduce yourself to these fine gentlemen?" Her uncle turned back toward her and put his enormous hands on his hips. Wisps of fire flitted across his opaque black pupils.

"Nope, I thought you'd do it so much better than I ever could."

The demons quivered when her uncle turned his full stare on them. He drew himself up to his full height, which nearly reached the ceiling, and his dark red body expanded.

"My niece summoned me. My niece never summons me unless something is wrong, or she wants a bedtime story read to her. And since she's not five years old anymore, that means something's wrong." His voice exploded through the room, shaking the windows.

The child next to the dead woman cried harder and Sara stepped around her uncle, walked over and scooped the child into her arms. He clung to her and buried his face into her shoulder. His damp curls stuck to her sweater. She shot a glare at the demons and sauntered back over to her uncle.

The child's guardian angel looked at the demons, at Sara and Beelzebub, then up toward heaven. Shuddering, the angel crept past the demons and stood near Sara. After shivering one more time, it bowed its head and began to move its lips in silent prayer.

Sara rolled her eyes and held the child tighter. Her uncle Bub gave a small shake of his head and rolled his eyes toward the ceiling. Sara was pretty sure she got her eye rolling tendencies from him. She also had a sneaking suspicion the guardian angel was only allowed to stay because of her.

"This lovely, wonderful, incredible, amazing—" Beelzebub intoned, looking down at his niece.

"B!" Sara interrupted him with a smack to the chest. The two demons gave each other a puzzled look before snapping their attention back to the huge demon.

"As I was saying," her uncle glanced at her to ensure he wouldn't be interrupted again, then back at the two smaller demons, "this young woman here is Lucifer's daughter, the anti-Christ."

"Uncle Bub, you know I'm not really the anti-Christ." Sara disregarded his stern gaze and interrupted his introduction yet again.

"Yes, you are, honey." Her uncle wrinkled his brow and tilted his head at her.

"Well, not really. Not the one that books are written about and movies made of," she argued. "I'm the daughter of Satan that cried when other little demons beheaded my cabbage patch dolls. Remember how you used to sew their heads back on for me? The four horsemen sigh and shake their heads at me still. They check in with me from time to time, but everyone knows I'm the 'anti' anti-Christ."

"Plus," she went on, "if I strike against a demon, score one point for the army of Heaven. If I strike against an angel, the soldiers of Hell cheer. I'm damned if I do and damned if I don't. Well, actually I'm damned anyways." She grinned up at him.

Her uncle tilted his head at her and looked at the ceiling. He appeared to be counting to ten. It was a common occurrence in her presence. She widened her smile.

"I don't know about all that, but an apocalypse might be fun." He scrunched his face and returned her smile.

She smacked him and giggled.

"No," she said.

"All right, then, let's get this dog and pony circus on the road." Her uncle reached out and tapped her on the chin. "Take care, little Sara bean." She nodded at him, afraid that if she spoke, she'd start crying and that would only complicate the moment more. Her throat was clogged with emotion and she was already drained.

Beelzebub turned back to the smaller demons, still cowering in confusion. Their cocky, arrogant manner had disappeared. Sara had no doubt her uncle was going to take them to a special place in Hell and set them up with an awesomely dreadful itinerary for the next millennium.

"You think you can break the chain of command, do you?" his fiery velvet voice crooned at them, promising them torture unimaginable for their breach of conduct.

"No, sir, no, we did not." The smaller of the demons splayed his bloody hands at his prince. His wide eyes turned up and the inky depths shimmered in fear.

"Well, let me show you what happens to those that violate it," Beelzebub's voice boomed through the room and he reached toward the two. Their bodies started to twist and contort. Bones snapped. Their shrill screams of pain echoed against the rafters.

The boy in Sara's arms tightened his hold. She held him closer and ignored the gasps of his guardian angel.

"Uncle B, before you go, would you send a minor dominion of Hell to help watch over this little boy? His guardian angel needs a little assistance." She shot a glare at the boy's angel.

Her uncle continued to contort the demons. "Sure, Sara, consider it done." Then both he and the demons were gone.

Sara smoothed the child's soft hair and stepped over pieces of broken chair. At the door, she gave a quick look back at the corpse. The police would never solve this crime. There would be no fingerprints, no DNA other than mother and child's, and no evidence to assist in the investigation. It would remain a baffling cold case file.

The child would always carry the scars of this night, but with both a guardian angel and now a minor demon, the scales would hopefully be balanced and give him the best shot at a decent future. He'd have his own internal demons, but a demon charged with his protection would keep away larger and more terrifying ones.

"I'm sorry, kiddo," she whispered to the child. Had she acted in the mother's defense and struck out against the demons sooner, the young woman might still be alive. Yet that decision would have led to a larger one.

Today wasn't the day to start an apocalypse.

The Exclusive, True History of Dick Cheney, George W. Bush and the Secret Neocon Plan to Get into Heaven

Roger Barr

A chance statement in early 2001 by a lower-level budget analyst working in the White House set into motion one of the more bizarre and secret initiatives of the George W. Bush administration, according to a former White House official, speaking publicly here for the first time. The official directly implicated then-Vice President Dick Cheney and indirectly linked President Bush himself to a bold plan to gain entry into heaven that encompassed most of Mr. Bush's first term.

The official spoke only after being assured of anonymity. "Look what happened to Joseph Wilson in 2003," the official told this reporter. "They outed his wife Valerie Plame as a CIA agent because Wilson was critical of the Administration's policy on Iraq. Think what could happen if someone determined I was the one who leaked a story about Bush and his minions trying to pull the wool over God's eyes."

"Just call me Deep Six," the official said, playing off of "Deep Throat," the legendary anonymous source who exposed abuses of power within the Nixon White House to *Washington Post* journalist Bob Woodward during the Watergate era. "As in inches, not feet. After all, it's what Bush ultimately did to the country for eight years."

The official left the administration in early 2005, before President Bush began his second term. "I decided to leave when all that 'moral values' stuff came after the 2004 election," Deep Six said. "As a Rockefeller-style Republican, I had been unhappy for a long time, but that was the straw that broke the camel's back, so to speak. I mean, it was presumptuous of them to assume they had only the small matter of their wealth to finesse through the gates of heaven, as if they themselves could pass through the morality checkpoint like it was a TSA gate at the airport!"

According to Deep Six, to understand the initiative, it is necessary to start not at the beginning, but with the end. The time is near, says the Book of Revelation, when all the dead will be raised up and judged. Those whose names are recorded in the book of life will enjoy eternal life while the rest descend for all time into the lake of fire.

The rising influence of Christian fundamentalism in federal policy has been well documented in other articles and books. The contested 2000 election marked the culmination of the rise of the Neoconservatives to power. On Inauguration Day 2001, Democrats consoled themselves with the hope that George W. Bush would be the compassionate conservative he claimed to be during the campaign. But once in the White House, Bush made a hard right turn. With control of both houses of Congress and the White House, Neoconservatives seized the opportunity to remake the country in their own image. Social conservatives sought to return the country to its traditional Christian roots. Tax-hating Republicans pursued a return to pro-business policies.

The Republican agenda posed an interesting moral question: if the time was near, as social conservatives believe, why would fiscal Republicans be so focused on increasing their wealth through tax cuts, and other aspects of the Bush economic policy that benefit the rich? After all, you can't take it with you when you go. Or can you?

Creating Reality

No other president in recent history seemed more determined to redefine not just the political landscape but reality itself. Not until 2005, at least, had any recent president been so successful. Whether it was labeling his domestic policies that favored the rich at the expense of the poor as "compassionate conservatism" or justifying the invasion of Iraq in 2003 with intelligence that was questioned at the time and later fully discredited, the Bush Administration consistently defined a reality, stuck to it and operated within it.

The Bush Administration's propensity to create its own reality was succinctly explained by a "senior advisor to the president" to *New York Times* journalist Ron Suskind, in a 2004 meeting where Suskind was chastised by the senior advisor for his reporting. According to Suskind, "The aide said that guys like me (Suskind) were 'in what we call the reality-based community,' which [the senior advisor] defined as people who 'believe' that 'solutions emerge from your judicious study of discernible reality.'" The senior advisor, later identified as Karl Rove, went on to tell Suskind, "That's not the way the world really works anymore. We're an empire now, and when we act we create our own reality."

In the manner of the Monroe or Truman Doctrines, we might call this the Empire Doctrine.

It was a biblical story involving the humble camel that led to one of the most bizarre domestic applications of the Empire Doctrine. According to Deep Six, the initiative began in early 2001 as the White House was putting together its economic package, which included extensive tax cuts. In the weeks following the inauguration, the president's economic advisors were gathered to hammer out the last details of the president's tax package. An assortment of analysts, economists and aides were assembled around a conference table roughly the size of an aircraft carrier. Meticulously, an analyst went through the proposal point by point.

Never one to spend time on details, the president interrupted.

"What's the overall impact?"

Knowing President Bush's fundamentalist tendencies and seeing the opportunity to score brownie points, the analyst leaned forward earnestly and clasped his hands together.

"Basically, Mr. President, if passed by Congress, the impact of the legislation is that it will be even harder for the top one percent of us to get into heaven." The analyst leaned back in his chair, pleased with himself.

No slouch in his knowledge of the scriptures, the president nodded, his brow furrowed. "Well, that is a problem." He turned to the vice president. "Dick, take care of that."

Around the table, everyone looked at each other and then looked away. Bush's conservative religious views were well known. Had the president really just ordered his vice president to figure out a way to get the top one percent of the population and all their wealth into heaven? No one dared ask a question to clarify. No one dared refuse to carry out an order.

Only the vice president seemed unfazed. "Certainly, Mr. President," Cheney said, making a note on the yellow legal pad in front of him. "I'll get right on it."

Among the assembled, there was a shifting of positions, of looking and then not looking at one another. But no one said a word. No one cracked even the hint of a smile. Such is the power of the presidency. Shortly thereafter, the meeting ended and the vice president did the equivalent of wadding up his notes and dropping the yellow ball of paper into the wastebasket. The incident was quickly forgotten. Months went by.

Then one of the vice president's staff buttonholed a junior staff member in the hallway. "Get me some background on these subjects," the senior staffer said. He handed the junior staffer a page from a yellow legal pad. There were two words written on it: "needles" and "camels."

The junior staffer later showed the yellow page to Deep Six. "He ordered me to assign this to a couple of interns," he told Deep Six. "He said to keep them apart and give the results only to him. What do you think it's about?"

"At first I was puzzled," Deep Six recalled. "What did camels have to do with politics? Donkeys and elephants I understood, but camels? It took until the next day for me to make the connection back to the meeting. I couldn't believe it! Someone actually saw a problem that needed to be fixed, and it fell upon Cheney's office to devise a solution."

And, exactly, what was the problem? The camel and the needle story appears in the gospels of Matthew, Mark and Luke, indicating that Jesus and/or the writers of the gospels, considered its lesson to be of central importance to being a Christian.

The three versions of the story are very similar. A man asks Jesus how to achieve eternal life. In each version, Jesus tells the questioner to obey the commandments. In Matthew 19:20, the man assures Jesus that, "All these I have observed; what do I still lack?" Jesus replies, "If you would be perfect, go, sell what you possess and give to the poor, and you will have treasure in heaven; and come, follow me."

According to Matthew 19:22, "When the man heard this he went away sorrowful; for he had great possessions." Following the man's departure, Jesus said to the disciples, "It will be hard for a rich man to enter the kingdom of heaven. Again I tell you, it is easier for a camel to go through the eye of a needle than for a rich man to enter the kingdom of God." (Matthew 19:23-24)

In Luke 18:18, the text identifies the man who questions Jesus on the route to heaven as a "ruler," a term that could give pause to a president who may have considered the Bible as literal truth.

Ideologues adapt reality to their own beliefs. Rather than turning "away sorrowful," President Bush either deliberately or inadvertently set into motion a plan where the Empire Doctrine was applied to alter New Testament reality to his beliefs.

Former Vice President Cheney, when contacted and asked for comment on the subject, gave this reporter the same advice he once gave Democratic Senator Patrick Leahy on the Senate floor.

In retrospective, we can reconstruct the arc, if not the exact steps, of the vice president's thought processes. Every problem has a solution. The problem is simple: how do you get the camel through the eye of the needle?

The camel was one of God's creatures. The needle was a manmade object. It could simply be changed, made larger—much larger—to accommodate a camel. The camel could pass through the eye of the needle and the problem of how a rich man could get into heaven would be solved.

With the basic concept in place, a memo was prepared summarizing the project. Deep Six saw a copy of the memo that later disappeared. According to the memo, with the plan properly executed, "On the great role of the dice, we should be able to leave Park Place or Boardwalk, pass GO and collect our $200, as it were."

In other words, take it with you. The camel through the eye of the needle project became known by the code name "PG/200."

Follow the Camel

An intern in the Department of Commerce was assigned a research project on needles under the pretext of preparation for an international trade show. An intern working for the Department of the Interior was assigned the research on camels, for "background" on an upcoming recognition of the U.S. Army's ill-fated efforts in the mid-nineteenth century to use camels as cavalry animals in the arid American southwest.

The actual research of both interns has disappeared from the archival files of Commerce and Interior. However, Internet searches produced documented year-end celebrations of the departments' internship programs that listed the interns' names and research topics.

The intern assigned to the Department of Interior who conducted the research on camels requested anonymity, referring to himself as "Joe Camel." The intern who conducted research on needles for the Department of Commerce referred to himself as "Mr. Singer," after the sewing machine company.

Joe Camel and Mr. Singer never met and never knew of each other's work. Expressly forbidden from keeping copies of their research, the former interns shared what they could remember, and additional research and fact checking has verified their accounts.

According to Joe Camel, his assignment was to learn all he could about camels, should the Camel Cavalry recognition want to do any kind of reenactment. Recalling his research, he described the camel as "a curious animal in the annals of history." Domesticated centuries ago, the animal known as "the ship of the desert" is not one of God's most graceful creations. There is a joke in the corporate world that the camel is a horse designed by a committee.

One of the sources Joe Camel used was Hans Biedermann's 1989 *Dictionary of Symbolism*. According to that publication, in the fourth and fifth centuries A.D., St. Augustine made the camel a symbol for the humble Christian shouldering life's burden without complaint, a stark irony to the motivations behind PG/200. Biedermann further notes that the camel has also been used symbolically to portray arrogance and selfishness, a usage more in keeping with the project at hand.

As directed, Joe Camel researched leads to purchasing a camel on the Internet, uncovering a host of websites associated with the burgeoning camel industry in this country. He assembled an annotated list of websites, which he attached to his final paper. His internship completed, he graduated from college and began to look for a job in the soft economy.

Calls made to the names on Joe Camel's annotated list yielded one dealer who recalled an unusual transaction. The dealer produced his copy of a bill of sale for a single camel to an animal trainer for $8,000 cash in August of 2003. The document included the trainer's name and address.

After being shown the document, the trainer confirmed that he had purchased and trained a camel for clients who said they were making a movie and paid cash. Over a period of several weeks, he trained the camel to accept a single, then a double hobble, to "cush" or lie down, and finally to step through a space whose measurements would later match exactly the dimensions for the eye of a gigantic manufactured needle.

The Needle in the On-line Haystack

Like Joe Camel, Mr. Singer turned in his research, completed his internship and had no further connection to PG/200. His research provided an outline for the manufacture of a single needle of gigantic dimension.

An Internet search produced no references to the alleged trade show. However, halfway through a list of 24,000 hits for the term "gigantic needle," the following annotation appeared: "The industrial artist Gusto created a gigantic needle for a trade show that was never held, but photos of his work can be viewed at the artist's website."

Gusto proved more than happy to talk about his art. "It was a commission," he recalled. "I was signed to a confidential contract. They gave me a household needle and asked me to create a gigantic needle that looked just like it. There were only two specifications: The dimensions of the eye had to be eight feet. And the needle needed to be in sections so it could be dismantled for travel."

Gusto determined that to create an eight-foot eye of a needle, the needle itself would have to be approximately 150 feet long.

Gusto decided to construct the needle from sections of corrugated metal culverts six feet in diameter used in civil engineering projects. He purchased 150 feet of culvert in ten-foot sections that easily bolted together. At one end, he smashed the culvert flat and cut the eye into the flattened metal with an acetylene torch. With considerable effort, he was able to cut and shape the opposite end into a point that approximated the point of the household needle.

His patron took delivery of the objet d'art in April 2004. Once paid his commission, Gusto heard no more about the project. "I kept asking when the show would be, but kept getting the runaround," Gusto told this reporter. "Finally I received word that the show had been canceled, but not to worry, since I had been paid the full commission. Fortunately, I had taken pictures of the project, even though I wasn't supposed to. When they said the trade show had been canceled, I thought, what the hell, the confidentiality had been nullified. I posted the pictures in the gallery on my website."

The First Test

According to Deep Six, the camel and the needle were brought together for the first time in late August of 2004. The gigantic needle was assembled and positioned horizontally to the ground, held stationary by X-shaped wooden frames. A test was scheduled for September 1, by coincidence, the same day as the first of the three debates between President Bush and the Democratic challenger, John Kerry.

Before the camel was even brought out, a design flaw was discovered in the needle. Gusto had indeed incorporated the required eight-foot dimension into the construction, but he had oriented the dimension to the length of the needle's eye, rather than its width. As the needle was positioned, the eight-foot dimension was parallel to the ground, rather than perpendicular, which it needed to be for an upright camel to pass through. The test was canceled until project leaders figured out what to do. The project manager glumly went off to deliver the bad news.

According to Deep Six, the president found out about the failed test minutes before going on stage for the debate. Exactly how the news affected him may never be known, but archival video of the debate shows the president angry, poorly prepared and outpointed by his rival. Contemporary newspaper accounts described the president as petulant.

The first presidential debate is often regarded as the low point of Bush's 2004 campaign, and perhaps the weakest moment of his first term.

It was back to the drawing board. New calculations were made. To make the narrow part of the eye wide enough for the camel to pass through while the needle was positioned horizontal to the ground would require a needle 300 feet long. It would set the project back months to design and manufacture such a needle.

Project managers focused their attention on the needle they had rather than the needle they wanted. The idea that the camel could be trained to crawl through the eye was raised and rejected. At this point, one of the workers observed that the Bible passages did not specify that it was a living camel that had to pass through the needle's eye. If the camel were rendered unconscious, perhaps permanently, it could be dragged through the needle's eye by a chain hooked to a Humvee. This suggestion was neither rejected nor approved.

It was suggested that if the current needle could somehow be stood on end so that the eight-foot dimension of the needle's eye was perpendicular to the ground, the camel could step right through it. It did not seem feasible to dig a hole wide and deep enough so that just the eye of the needle stuck out of the ground. Rather, the needle could be suspended by its point from a building crane, the end with the eye just touching the ground.

This decision necessitated moving the test site to another location where a ten-story crane could be erected without causing suspicion. A site in Texas was identified for the new test. For cover, a story was developed that the site was being prepared for a new oil well, but the finances had fallen apart, ending the project. The new plan delayed the test until late fall while the crane was secured, transported to the site and erected.

The Final Test

A new test was scheduled for late November, following the presidential election. On the morning of the test, a small group of workers made their way to the site, where others had labored through the night to bolt the needle together. From a distance, silhouetted against the morning sky, the object indeed looked like a giant needle hanging by its point, its eye swaying just above the ground. Light was visible through the eye of the needle, the light at the end of the tunnel, as it were.

The camel was unloaded from its trailer and led to the needle. The great moment had arrived. But a new problem arose. The easiest way to get the camel through the needle was to lead it through. Although none of the crew admitted to being superstitious, no one volunteered to step through the eye of the needle, leading the camel behind him. The problem was solved when the reins were lengthened so they could be handed from one crewmember to the other in such a way that no one had to actually pass through the needle's eye.

The camel, however, balked at the idea of passing through a narrow space with metal on either side when a few feet in either direction he could walk unencumbered. Workers tried to blindfold the camel. The camel would have none of that.

After much discussion, a wooden frame was quickly erected on either side of the needle, and sections of blue polyethylene tarpaulins were lashed to the frame, in effect transforming the eye of the needle into a doorway through a wall of blue.

The camel was led toward the opening again. A man on the other side reached through to accept the reins and pull the camel through the space. At that point a gust of wind caught one corner of the tarpaulin that was poorly secured. The tarp snapped in the wind and startled the camel, which reared back, broke free from its handlers, and with its stiff-legged gait galloped off into the Texas sunset. The crew looked at the rear end of the retreating camel and then at each other.

A crewmember reached into his shirt pocket and removed a new pack of Camel cigarettes. He opened the pack, shook one out and lit it. He took a deep drag and exhaled the smoke slowly. Taking another drag, he flicked the burning cigarette through the needle's eye. "Tell whoever you are working for that the Camel has passed through the eye of the needle," he said.

The assembled looked at each other. The whole thing was a scam. What was one more? Word was passed up the chain of command that the mission had, at last, been accomplished, the camel had easily passed through the eye of the needle and those that mattered could pass GO and collect their $200.

The Democrats Fail to Capitalize

Rumors about PG/200 circulated within the upper echelons of the Democratic Party as early as June of 2004. When these rumors first circulated, the Democratic Party immediately launched a quiet investigation of its own. Researchers were able to confirm basic facts, but found that, like other issues, key records were missing from government sources.

Party leaders, according to an informed source who refused to be named, suspected the handiwork of presidential advisor Karl Rove.

"We were cautious," the source admitted years later. "Every time we dealt with the Bush cabal we had to be watchful that we weren't being set up." Any thoughts the Democrats had during the 2004 campaign about exposing PG/200 for political advantage were scuttled in the wake of the Swift Boat Veterans for Truth incident. In a matter of days, a withering campaign orchestrated by the organization Swift Boat Veterans for Truth transformed Democratic presidential candidate John Kerry from a genuine war hero into a suspected traitor. The Swift Boat claims were later debunked, but they severely damaged Kerry's candidacy.

On the heels of the Swift Boat claims, a CBS Network news story critical of President Bush's own service record was discredited. The Bush campaign successfully cast doubt on the authenticity of several records CBS used in preparation of the story. As a result, the authenticity of the documents and the political motives of CBS became the story instead of the president's service record. The scandal eventually accelerated the retirement of CBS's veteran news anchor and "60 Minutes" correspondent Dan Rather.

Democrats were also stymied during much of the 2004 campaign by faith issues. "Democrats don't know how to claim the faith issue," one official on the Democratic National Committee admitted after the election. "The conservatives have somehow convinced the country that only Republicans believe in God."

In the end, fearing the worst if they took any action, Democrats failed to capitalize on the political opportunities PG/200 offered.

Democrats were not the only ones to give PG/200 a free pass. Until this article, the issue has received virtually no press. In 2004, the shadow of 9/11 still fell across the computer screens and television cameras of the mainstream media. In the months following 9/11, politicians and journalists alike were careful not to criticize policy for fear of dishonoring those whose lives were lost in the terrorist attacks. The Bush Administration was extremely successful in capitalizing on this sentiment and institutionalizing it. To criticize the administration or one of its policies became, in a word, unpatriotic.

Following the 2004 election, the PG/200 story was pitched unsuccessfully to several of the nation's leading news magazines. All passed. One editor who requested anonymity admitted that the press was cautious about investigative reporting in the wake of the CBS scandal.

"Times have changed," the editor said. "We're not just looking for the smoking gun anymore. We want the gun in someone's hand. We want the body. We want an autopsy report that the victim died of gunshot wounds. And we want test results confirming that the smoking gun was the gun that actually killed the victim."

The Bush Administration never acknowledged the existence of PG/200. In 2014, a draft of this article was sent to the George W. Bush Library requesting comment but no response was ever received. Even though the former president has remained silent on the subject of PG/200, he now knows that the mission was not accomplished, that the only camel that passed easily through the eye of a needle was supplied, albeit unknowingly, by Big Tobacco.

We can assume that in one form or another PG/200 will be back as long as someone believes there is a problem and uses this episode as a blueprint for future solutions. After all, the time is near.

Monkey Man

Charley B. Murphy

My husband has begun to really frighten me.

Brief background. We live in an ex-urban suburb of St. Paul, Minnesota. We are an older couple, married forever, one grown and married daughter who pretty much lets us be, thank God. I'm still working, at least for another decade, given the way things are at my job as a high school guidance counselor. Which you can imagine is pretty depressing. Don't follow your dreams like my befuddled generation and all that. My husband recently retired (he's older than me and had a pension) from his job in new product development at a very large consumer products company, which I won't mention by name lest some of their lawyers are listening. They do that. Some of my girlfriends (yes, we use that term) tell me his behavior is all about him adjusting to retirement. Fine, I say, for a hypothesis, I need an action plan. And soon.

Joseph always had plenty of interests outside of work and family, so retirement wasn't scary in the sense of not knowing what to do. More the opposite. At one time, he imagined he could have been a professor of anthropology, but he was too eclectic and intolerant of politics to make it in academia. He's one of these Discovery Channel nuts, can't get enough of every offbeat show on UFOs and ancient civilizations, Nazi occultism, and his favorite—cryptozoology.

If you don't have a husband like Joseph, you may be one of the 99 percent who don't know or don't care about the "study of evidence tending to substantiate the existence of, or the search for, creatures whose reported existence is unproven, as the Abominable Snowman or the Loch Ness Monster."

Joseph would hate Dictionary.com's avoidance of the term Yeti. I mean even I know not to use Abominable Snowman. Who were they abominable to? But there you have it, more background than you might need.

Now, here's what's going on.

We own four wooded acres on a swampy little Minnesota Lake. Our house is set back from the road and our driveway is long and graveled. I'd say we are a fairly "liberated" couple as far as gender stereotypes go. Like many couples our age, we found it easier to rely on how we were raised as far as who does what chore. Joseph grills the meat, deals with the cars, and takes out the garbage. I'm not saying he doesn't do other things, but I wanted to get to that last chore, which is the focal point of what I want to tell you about.

I'll walk you through it.

It was a full moon or close to one, maybe just a sliver to one side or the other of waxing or waning. Joseph left the house about ten p.m., was gone the customary ten minutes plus or so. When he returned, he looked ashen.

"What happened?" I asked from my chair, where I was enjoying a cup of chamomile tea.

He looked around almost furtively, possibly embarrassed. I got out of my chair and walked over to him. Getting out of my chair is not a small deal when I have a fresh cup of tea and my Kindle all revved up and ready to go with the first book of a decent trilogy of women's fiction.

"Chamomile tea?" I asked almost cruelly. He hates chamomile tea. It was my way of saying sit down and tell me what happened.

He slumped on the couch, staring straight ahead, rubbing his hand on his bald head like he used to when he had hair. The nervous habit outlived the follicles. "Yeah, sure," he said, which is when I started to think something medical had occurred, because Joseph saying yes to chamomile tea is like a five-year-old saying he's ready for his nap now.

I gave him the cup and he held it with trembling hands. Why was he shaking?

"You know how I am," he stated.

I looked at him steadily. It was a loaded understatement. Do I ever know how he is?

"I play with my mind," he said.

The phrase mental masturbation came to me, but I quickly cast it out. I don't even like using the word masturbation with my students. Boy, do they know that word and all its conjugations.

"Go on," I said, nodding, like a licensed therapist, which I am not.

"Well, you know, I've told you before. There were times when I thought I saw something, you know, in the forest."

"Something," I said with flat affect, treating him like a troubled teen. Truth is he's been seeing things in the woods for months, maybe longer. But he used to tell me about them like he would a particularly vivid dream, sort of proud of his imagination. Like a child saying he saw a dinosaur in the mall to impress you.

"You know, a cryptid."

Sadly, I know a cryptid is an imaginary monster. Yeti, Loch Ness, et cetera. This was one of Joseph's many incomprehensible hobbies as I had begun to tell you. Joseph loved to watch these shows that pretend to be reality shows, guys tracking Bigfoot, always ending on almost finding evidence. Can they really call these reality shows? I guess it's the reality of being obsessed.

As I was thinking these thoughts I sat and waited for his next statement.

He was staring at me like he knew I was disparaging him in my mind. But I held my gaze steady. I've had practice with young people telling me all sorts of things. Some overtly supernatural, thank you very much, pop culture. I've heard about devils, demons, conjurations, pentagrams, they love to try to shock me. Like I haven't seen *Nightmare on Elm Street*. If you exclude the vampires and werewolves they imagine their ex-lovers to be, I don't really deal with your mainstream cryptids.

"So..." he started but looked away. "I've seen it before, but I thought I was making it up. I know what you call it."

I think I succeeded in not smiling. Oh, I'm good.

"This time, I walked into the forest but I had to look where I was walking." We encouraged each other to look where we walk, especially in forests. Tripping and falling for anyone over fifty isn't a pratfall. Bones don't heal as quickly anymore.

"When I looked up, I felt foolish because I couldn't see *it* anymore. I turned around to head back to the driveway but I heard a noise."

"A noise," I said, trying to appear fully engaged, fully believing.

"Like a growl or maybe a growly language."

When he said, "growly language," I almost smirked.

"When I looked up again, Marian, I'm telling you God's awful truth—he was looking right at me."

I was flooded with potential responses. Some, you might say, were a stand-up comedian's (and I'm not really a funny person, though I do enjoy the occasional wisecrack). Some were a psychologist's. My wifely response needed full-on repression, as it was something along the lines of "Jesus fucking Christ, get some help already." All these potential reactions went through my mind. Hopefully my face remained straightforwardly attentive and interested with a touch of comradely concern (versus wifely panic, judgment, and outright ridicule). Being a guidance counselor has its benefits.

"He said..." Joseph said.

He spoke? The Thing in the Forest spoke? "What did he say, hon?" In his comprehensible, growly language.

"He said he had chosen me."

"Chosen you for what?"

I knew Joseph well enough to know that being chosen resonated at a deep level. For his entire life, he felt he had been somewhat unappreciated—a fish out of water, an animal placed in the wrong wing of the zoo. What great work or destiny he wanted to be or imagined himself to be chosen for, I wasn't sure I wanted to know.

"He said it would involve a violent act."

This quieted me down. Way down. My husband wasn't a violent man. He once tried to become a hunter and ended up crying (okay, mourning, grieving) over anything he killed. Paul Bunyan would have snickered.

At this point, I became deeply concerned. A professional might be needed here. Medication. Possibly a locked ward like the asylum Olivia de Havilland occupied in *The Snake Pit*. I folded my hands to suppress my desire to touch him. I'm not sure why I was afraid. He was my husband, having a moment.

Just then the doorbell rang. Nobody rings the doorbell out here in the woods on a Sunday evening. I barely know my neighbors and it's too late for Jehovah's Witnesses. It could be a cop, I suppose, telling us about an escaped convict. Bayport Prison isn't that far away. It's not impossible.

I looked at Joseph. Normally a late-night caller would fall into the category of "men's jobs" not unlike the bump in the night that would require him to go downstairs with a baseball bat. As clichéd as that sounds, we do have a baseball bat under the bed.

One look at Joseph and I realized this task was suddenly in the care-taking wife's category. He looked like blood was draining from his face. I hadn't seen him look this limp and washed out since he got dehydrated after his colonoscopy.

"Okay," I said with only the slightest hint of displeasure. "I'll get it."

I went to the door and turned on the porch light. We don't have a peephole, just a strip of clear glass on either side of the door. Normally, if visitors wanted to be seen (especially at night) they would deliberately stand to the left or right of the solid oak door to make themselves visible, thus lessening the possible fright activated by the surprise of a nighttime caller.

But murderers don't ring doorbells. Plus, my husband, however rattled, was sitting right there. Even in his debilitated state, I'm sure he could rise to the occasion if a gruff criminal voice said anything off-color.

I opened the door and saw a smallish man in what appeared to be a realistic gorilla suit, only with a slight reddish cast to the fur. A ginger ape suit. I looked behind me, half-expecting Joseph to be standing behind me enjoying a laugh. I have to say that he's not much of a prankster, but with men you never know. I'm with Yoko Ono that their dangly genitalia makes them inherently funny.

"So what's the big joke?" I asked the ginger gorilla.

I took the time to admire his costume, especially where the mask met his eyes. I couldn't see any break where the plastic mask separated from the human flesh underneath. It was all super-realistic and reminded me of the time Joseph showed me the new CGI (he told me this means "computer generated imagery") in a remake of *Planet of the Apes*, one of his favorite films. He didn't care for the remake, but we both enjoyed the massive jumps they've made since the original *King Kong*, which scared me as a girl even though I knew it had to be stop-motion or claymation or whatever.

"Who is it?" Joseph yelled out. Like he didn't know.

"Your gorilla friend."

"My what?"

I heard sounds from the parlor, possibly a chair being turned over, then Joseph was standing next to me. He was really going to elaborate lengths on this. For a moment I wondered if it could be April Fool's Day. Yeah, in November? Even Halloween was way past. I wasn't crazy about it, but I married a joker. Some things you have to put up with.

I turned to look at Joseph with an expression that said, *Okay, fun's up, I'm getting tired.*

He looked worse than he had a moment ago. Paler, shakier. Open-mouthed, like an Alzheimer's patient who just realized he forgot his own name.

I turned back to look at our trick-or-treater (that's where my mind went) and he began to cock his head first one way then the other. Joseph tried to close the door on him but I was partially in the way and not about to move until I got an explanation. The prank was starting to get me crabby.

"He's..." Joseph struggled to form words. "He's real, Marian. Shut the goddamn door!"

I tried to shut the goddam door, as my dear, possibly insane husband instructed me, but slowly, not in a panic. I don't like being bossed around even in an emergency. I closed the door with deliberation like I had just told the Jehovah's Witnesses we were Satanist even though it was mainly Joseph's joke, not mine.

The man in the suddenly not-so-funny monkey suit put his foot in the door, and I admired the realistic hair on his costumed foot.

"Ouch," he said.

I turned to Joseph, looking for an explanation and feeling my eyebrows and even ears raised in alarm. He shook his head. Was it possible he was about to cry? That wasn't something he did often unless a dog died in a movie.

I turned angrily to the monkey man, opened the door a bit so it wasn't squishing his foot and said, "See here, young man..." I assumed he was a young man because most of the time these pranksters turn out to be young men. Still, I realized how sexist and reverse-agist that is.

"What do you want?" I asked rather harshly. "The joke's over, buster. It's late."

"Please let me in," he said. "Your husband..." He nodded toward Joseph as if he would deliver the rest of the explanation. But Joseph stepped back and put both hands to his mouth in a kind of girlish gesture and shook his head from side to side like he was auditioning for a horror movie.

"Oh, for Pete's sake," I said. "Let's have this out. What's this elaborate prank all about?" I wasn't afraid to let the monkey man see that I admired his costume. I could see he was male now. There was the male voice, of course, and also a fur-covered protuberance at his crotch, which I passed my eyes over quickly.

The monkey man spoke: "Your husband knows." His accent was not exactly Minnesota-Midwestern. Not exactly British either, kind of a theatrical stagey American dinner theater accent.

"Goddamn it, Joseph," I said. And you should know I'm not a swearing person unless I'm riled. "What's going on here?"

"No, no, no," he said backing up, nearly tripping on our fake Persian rug runner we got at Home Depot's online store.

I turned back to the monkey man. "Now see here…" I sounded like an old biddy in a 1950's sitcom scolding the Hardy Boys.

"Madame," Monkey Man said, "your husband called me forth. Conjured me from his subconscious, you might say. May I come in?"

"Of course," I said.

It was rude but I put a towel on the couch and indicated he could sit there. I didn't know where that rear end of his had been.

"Now, what's this all about? Are you some old frat buddy of Joe's?" Joseph hadn't been in a frat, so it was a trick question.

"May I smoke?"

"Of course not!"

"A little joke," Monkey Man said. "Joe, I think you should sit down."

Joseph walked over and sat in one of the two overstuffed chairs facing the couch. He walked stiffly, kept his hands covering his mouth the whole time. Some act, I thought.

"For heaven's sake, put your hands down," I directed. He obeyed. I turned back to Monkey Man and sat in my chair leaning forward just to show my level of unintimidatedness.

"Madame, you may want to sit down for this." Monkey Man laughed a little. Big joke. I was already sitting. "As you may or may not know, your husband here has been accessing powers of his mind that one might call 'loosely magical.' I prefer the more specific terms of classical Tibetan Buddhism, such as the manifestation of a tulpa."

"A tulpa," I repeated like I had heard the word before. Maybe I had. Maybe Joseph had rambled on about it once or twice when

I was hardly listening. I waited for Monkey Man to explain how he knew Joseph and give a reason as to why he would go to such great lengths to scare him. I began to think of Monkey Man as a kind of freelance therapist working outside the insurance structure on a mission reminiscent of the Yippies (I think that's what they called themselves from way back in my college days). They gave away free stuff and thought their antics would bring down western civilization. Who knows, maybe it had. Was I sitting across from a smallish Yippie who had grown up and become a freelance manifester of dreams, a sort of proactive one-man Make-A-Wish Foundation? I began to take a kinder tone with Monkey Man. He might be seriously disturbed. Possibly he had the wrong house.

"Would you like some tea? What should I call you?"

"That would be nice, ma'am. Very kind. My name is Garth. I'm an *Australopithecus afarensis*."

"Not a Big Foot? Sasquatch?" Joseph finally spoke.

Garth laughed. "I am only tangentially connected to cryptozoology, my friend. As you should well know."

"Why should I well-know that?" Joseph asked crabbily. "You walk in here, sit on my couch…"

Garth growled. Not like his language. Like a dog. "That line from Hamlet. There are more things in heaven and hell—"

"—than are dreamt of in your philosophy, Horatio. Ha, ha! Everyone knows that!" Joseph was talking in a way I had never heard him talk before. Like how a crazy person talks to himself in the alley when you walk by.

This might surprise you, but for the first time I started to feel afraid for Joseph. I was still working under the assumption that Garth was a man (as in human) especially now. Quoting Shakespeare only supported my hypothesis. But seeing his interaction with Joseph was disquieting. By that point, they should have been laughing and breaking out the bourbon, but Joseph remained nervous and had now become cranky. And he isn't a crabby man, not by a long shot. The grouchiness comes out only when he's sick. And he wasn't sick right then, other than starting to feel his years, which you might say is a form of sickness. Some people say that, but I think that's a very modern and rather un-ecological belief. Aging is just our exit ramp to death; it's not a sickness. How can aging be a sickness?

I remembered Garth or Mr. Garth had said yes to tea. I got up to give them time to decide how to present this all to me. Garth would pull off that realistic Yeti mask or whatever it was and I'd see his real face. I fully expected Joseph to get ahold of himself and properly introduce me on my return from the kitchen. I assumed that when I returned, they would have gotten over their strangeness. I expected to see an older man who was some sort of buddy or acquaintance of Joseph's, perhaps from college, who found my husband on Facebook and remembered this not-funny-Monkey-Man-arriving-unannounced-thing they always wanted to do but never did.

But as I was pouring the hot water into the cup, I felt my arthritis kicking in, especially in my hands. I was beginning to feel tired. The joke had gone on long enough. Even though he hadn't done so thus far, Mr. Garth would have to take off his mask to drink his tea. I took comfort in this—was ready for this nonsense to be over.

I walked back into a silent parlor. The two 'men' were barely looking at each other. I felt like I had walked in on a couple fighting. My confusion started changing into anger. I set the tea in front of Mr. Garth, who nodded in acknowledgment. He was as masked as ever.

"It was a… funny prank. A very funny prank."

Garth looked at me, confused. "Prank?"

"Yes. The suit." I indicated his outfit with my hand fluttering in his direction. "Your get-up."

"You don't understand, Marian," Joseph said. His voice sounded weird. Tired. Defeated. Like he had bet too much on poker and lost. "He's real. Some sort of manifestation of all my hopes and dreams, of contacting… I don't know, something mysterious. Bigfoot was as good as anything, I suppose, but he… You…" He shifted to address Garth. "That was never my favorite. I mean, if I had a choice—maybe aliens? I don't know."

"I'm not a Bigfoot, for chrissakes. I'm the very same *Australopithecus afarensis* you saw in the *Time Life* coffee table book your parents owned in 1958. Remember the picture of me hitting—no, killing—some lesser humanoid species with a thigh bone?"

"Like the apes in *2001*?" I offered helpfully. Nasty brutes, but clearly men in costumes.

"Yes," Garth said with some enthusiasm. "Stanley Kubrick probably saw the same picture in the same book." He looked as thoughtful as a man in a monkey mask could look. "Though he was a lot older than you."

"You're being kind," I said.

"No. He was born in 1928, if you can believe it."

Okay. Now you might ask why wasn't I afraid? I was talking to a small crazy person in an ape costume my husband apparently believed had sprung forth from his own subconscious. This made my husband crazy in a way I had never seen him before. Crazier than Monkey Man Garth in a way.

"Well, Mr. Garth…"

"Just Garth."

"Garth. It's my bedtime now, so I think it's time for this little party to be over. When you finish your tea, Joseph will see you to the door." I folded my hands. The queen had spoken.

"You don't understand," Garth said, suddenly agitated in tone. His body language changed, too. He started quivering like a dog when it sees a treat. I don't know how I had missed it, but he revealed a crudely chipped knife like you see in a museum display of Neolithic tools.

"It's time. It's *your* time. This was how *he* wanted it to happen."

"He? As in Joseph?" I was up and headed for the phone, 9-1-1 on my mind.

Joseph just shook his head sadly. "I'm sorry, Marian. I didn't know. I didn't know the world really worked this way."

Monkey Man quite nimbly (for an old man in that suit) leaped over the coffee table and with one large slashing motion sliced Joseph's throat. My husband leaned forward, gurgling in his own blood. He fought to talk.

"But this isn't my dream!" I screamed. "This isn't the way I saw it happening. Don't I get a say?"

"No. I'm afraid not," Garth said. "It doesn't work that way. I am Death and I have come for you." Garth approached me with that bloody, chipped obsidian knife.

I tried to run but was suddenly paralyzed for no reason. Like happens in a dream sometimes.

A Tasty Harvest for King Claudius

Bill Nemmers

Ross Crantz and Guilda Stern are but two of many Insertion Engineers working in our good King Claudius's Virtual-Dimension Laboratory. They do what they've been trained to do and they do it well. They surveil the little-bitty sub-atomic images dancing on their monitors. Well, no! Technically, that's not true. The images they are watching are computer generated reconstructions of what many of their colleagues think these sub-atomic images will look like if someone, sometime in the future, invents the technology that allows engineers to actually see them. I seriously doubt anyone will ever see them because they really are infinitesimally small—so small that their entire cosmic unity, containing untold billions of galaxies, can be, and in fact must be, stuffed into a container less than one electron-diameter across.

"Oh, wow, Ross. I can actually see those little humanoid thingies."

"Actually, Guilda, you can't see them. Even these hydrogen-powered micro-scanners can't zoom in close enough to distinguish individual organisms living on the surface of that little planet. These machines, however, do know exactly what those organisms are made of and how each of their atoms is arranged. But at such a micro-scale the entire idea of a visually identifiable dimension is meaningless. You only *sense* that virtual image dancing on your screen."

And so Guilda watches (or senses) virtual images of individual organisms romping through a certain time range and space environment and, to her, they look like real people doing real activities. She's still in training though, and not always able to distinguish real organisms from sympathetic reconstructions. Ross is training her to insert corrective synthetic probes into the tableau represented on her screen. Such corrections can be designed to keep the humanoid culture she is studying healthy. It's not rocket science, but it is tedious stressful work, loaded with extreme import and with the potential of causing catastrophic damage to the organism, if her insertions don't take.

"Armageddon is our goal, Guilda. We gotta maximize catastrophic effects. Then we grab the resulting flower just before the whole thing explodes." Ross, the cynic in the office, has a mobile of rainbow colored letters hanging above his desk proclaiming: *I do Instantaneous Armageddon.*

"It all depends which end of the microscope you're looking through." Ross loves this little story. "Except those humanoids on the small end have absolutely no idea that our instruments are trained on them. And that's understandable, since they have no conception of, nor even, I should think, metaphysical dreams about, our level of existence. Our time and space does not exist, for them at least. I know *they* exist but, from my perspective, I'm only able to see them because I'm comfortable with the fact that neither the time nor the space between us exists."

Everyone knows where this secret research facility, which our King Claudius built as a portal to *his* future, is located. It's in the mountains just south of Zurich. But only those who work here know *when* it is here, or what size it is when it is here. This must be so because, especially with respect to current experiments being done here, the theoretical dimensions of both size and time, *do not exist.* It's not that the microscopic sizes Guilda and Ross are dealing with are impossible to understand; it's that when working with structures at the extreme of rational understanding *size cannot physically exist.* It's impossible for even the very idea of size to exist. But a recognizable corollary does exist; if this size dimension either is so small it does not exist, or so large that it cannot exist, then the associate dimension—*time*—must not exist either. Essentially, this means that even though everyone knows King Claudius's facility is physically located in this suburban executive office park, it is not perfectly aligned with time and space such that no one not using their Secret-Holographic-Access-Reality-Key (SHARK) will ever be able to visually *see* it.

Earlier today, Ross, while viewing humanoid space/time through his hydrogen microscope, discovered an ideally situated planet located in the formation belt of the "Milky Way" galaxy. (It's possible Ross named this rich and rather gooey star-cluster after the candy bars he considers breakfast.) He gave responsibility for tracking the humanoid fungi growing on this little planet to his protégé, Guilda. He watches her successfully insert several probes into specific time slots in the fungal development growing on the planet's surface. Ross tells Guilda she must be careful because those humanoid fungi have a propensity to suddenly transform themselves into an uncontrollable machine-enhanced organism. And once humanoids adopt machines, the machines will turn on them and eventually destroy the humanoid fungi, and in most cases, the entire planet with it. Such a thermal-nuclear event will scatter much of the beautiful humanoid DNA into the hidden folds of the galactic cloud where it is, or soon will be, absorbed by any dark matter feeding there.

* * *

King Claudius's TROTI (Theoretical Reconstructions Of The Infinitesimal) engineers have learned that planetary humanoid fungi can be forced to develop naturally, i.e. without using science or machines. Such forcing requires Guilda or Ross to intervene, and their interventions can, in most—but not all—cases, ensure the *natural organic development* and eventually cause the quantity, or at least the volume, of the humanoid fungal life on the planet to accelerate asymptotically, to metamorphose naturally, and in the end—or immediately prior to the end—to transform itself into a harvestable bloom laden with pure unadulterated humanoid DNA.

TROTI has developed the process which allows such a bloom to be harvested at the peak of ripeness, just before it explodes on its own. Ross must pick that blossom prior to the explosion, and place it into refrigerated storage so other engineers can use the humanoid DNA to reinvigorate the amine compounds necessary for inoculating the good King Claudius and certain of his relatives and associates, and perhaps his subjects—specifically those laboring tirelessly in this lab for him—with fresh unadulterated (unadulterated by machines at least) humanoid DNA. The operation will, it is hoped, give him, them, and eventually all of us, immortality. This sequence assumes, of course, that some future time does, or soon will, exist.

* * *

Work at this small scale requires technical expertise, extreme patience, and an ability to strike quickly. It's often frustrating because they are able to successfully complete a harvesting only 30 percent of the time. Ross considers it a good day if his engineers harvest a dozen planets in the thirty-two hours the union allows them to work every day. Though Guilda and Ross realize their work is dangerous, both know that at this level of technical ambiguity any reasonable idea of 'danger' also *does not exist*. Once they leave the relative physical stability of their respective BMWs, now resting in full sight in the parking lot down by the reflecting pool, they must walk through the courtyard, transport themselves through the visually opaque entry portal of this facility, and enter the king's time-free zone.

Once inside, Guilda and Ross will be able to work without a need to separate various technical aspects of space and time. As any expert in the field of TROTI will tell you: if one has the proper security clearance and training, one can work comfortably in such virtual space and virtual time to harvest pure, uncontaminated, humanoid DNA from mega-microscopic level, space-time farming phenomena.

* * *

But all life is inherently dangerous. And the specific danger existing here in this time and space, is King Claudius's stepson, the Strange Prince. The Strange Prince has been infected by the so-called Crusade Virus, a disease originally developed with the help of the Vatican several centuries earlier. He's been radicalized by Armageddonist clerics from Texas, where he spent his youth and so for the last several years he's been doing anti-scientific jihad in several poor mid-eastern countries. Even though he is now a jihad-priest, he's one sneaky guy and Ross's TROTI lab must be continuously on the alert for the prince who, with his Spanish Inquisition (a motley crew of evil-smelling armed thugs) has been scouring the countryside with the intention of destroying all the machines owned by his father, the king.

Ross doubts the Strange Prince and his Spanish Inquisition will be able to find his visually-non-existent TROTI facility. It is quite invisible to those without proper passports. Plus, no one in the Kingdom takes the Strange Prince and his silly Spanish Inquisition too seriously. Though he is a supreme nuisance, everyone knows that: first, the Strange Prince and his group are as stupid as dirt clods; second, they've sworn off using technology and machines like GPS, motor vehicles and nuclear IEDs; and third, they have lost track of time, meaning they haven't yet been able to find the exit portal from the fifteenth century. So no one, including Ross, expects the Strange Prince to show up with his Spanish Inquisition and ruin things in his precisely located—with respect to time and place—TROTI laboratory.

* * *

Guilda's been working to harvest DNA from planets growing in the galaxy Ross has named after his favorite candy bar. She's been training hard on the hydrogen microscope and has raised her fast-twitch-muscle profile into the top tier. She's not quite a superstar yet but maybe, in a year—a profoundly inexact quantity for a TROTI lab—she will qualify as a team leader. She's a bit upset with herself because she'd done a rather clumsy job of inserting the traditional first-stage probe, the one code-named Noah. She watches as Noah's Flood-of-Retribution kills most all animal and vegetable life. The clumsy fool forgot to take her finger off the button! She should have been paying closer attention. "I'm sorry, Ross. I'm afraid it's gonna take hundreds of thousands of earth-years to recover from that."

"Not to worry, Guilda," Ross tells her. "Eventually the stupid fungi recover and that allows a healthy humanoid colony to reestablish itself. You'll have better luck next time!" Ross says that even though they both know: *time does not exist.*

Eventually, as they both anticipate, another alarm sounds, indicating Guilda's machine recognizes a common rogue virus, one Ross has labeled "The Aristotle Strain" which is threatening to introduce scientific thoughts into the intellectual stagnation introduced earlier by the Noahic probe. Guilda quickly reviews the weapons in her arsenal, then chooses one and inserts a second probe; this one she rams into a hillside near Jerusalem on a summer afternoon in 32 AD. This probe, named "Jesus," can work miracles and do other non-physical things to quite effectively obliterate science. Whereas the Noah probe did its work with cataclysm, this Jesus probe will use a reasonably nonviolent path to stifle intelligent scientific thought.

* * *

Jesus sits on a bare rock outcrop set atop a grass-covered mound. He looks down on thousands of poor, hungry, diseased and/or stupid humanoids, many of whom have been expelled—precisely because they are poor, hungry, diseased and/or stupid—from the walled city rising up like a giant machine above the forested landscape behind them. Though this Jesus has powers to feed, enfranchise, and politically empower the miscreants assembled before him, the first thing he must do is feed them. They'll never accept his argument on an empty stomach. Only after the grumbling and the belching quiets down, is he able to preach enfranchisement.

"My dear friends," he says. "The Roman pigs have Aristotle to guide their thoughts. They have engineers to build their palaces, scientists to construct their machines, soldiers to maintain compliance, and executioners to exterminate the unwanted. But you must not be afraid. Their machines may overpower you today, and even tomorrow, but on the next day, or the next after that, I will make them go away.

"You must know that you are my chosen ones. You are my precious sheep and, like sheep, you must follow me. And if you do, I will give you everlasting life. That means time, for you, *will not exist*. Four or five hundred years into your future, there will be no Romans, and so you, and your sons and daughters, will control the levers of this earth. And you will be free of the need for engineers, and scientists, and soldiers. I will guide you."

Jesus points up toward the sun or perhaps the blue firmament above it, and says, "Our Father, who art in heaven, hallowed be His name! He will bring you into his kingdom, if you do his will. He will give you your daily bread, if you do his will. He will forgive you your daily complaints as you must forgive your brethren. He will protect you from the evil Romans. All you have to do is follow me, and do what I say. Only then will you live happily. And, you shall live *happily forever*."

* * *

Jesus's effervescent and irrepressible intervention usually will sustain a slow growth over a long term and provide relief for several millennia. However, in this case, Guilda senses trouble after only fourteen-hundred years have passed. Another virus, a joint infestation of Florentine humanists and Renaissance artists has allowed the long-lost, scientifically based "Aristotle Strain" information to creep back into society from the rubble piles of the old Roman Empire. The scientific and artistic infections inflicted by these revitalized strains will, if left unchecked, again bond fungi to machine and threaten the long-term health of that humanoid fungi.

"Damn it, Ross," says Guilda, "I think we've got to intervene on your little blue planet again. That Jesus probe didn't work so well this time. Those damn humanists seem on the verge of destroying the Great Metaphysical Construct, thus laying bare the physical secrets of the universe. Once they figure out the science, they can use their humanoid intellect to resolve nature's many questions. It'll take them only a millennium or two to rebuild the Roman machines, and then they will ruin your pretty planet."

"Wow, that was a quick turnaround."

"What's wrong with Jesus? I wonder why his intervention didn't work here? Our time is running out fast."

"No big deal! Ya win some and ya lose some! And remember, dear Guilda: Time does not exist so it can't *run out*."

"What's the best way to kill that Renaissance virus?"

"You could send in the Spanish Inquisition," suggests Ross. "They usually do a bang-up job. Shit, Guilda! You see that?" He points to the information now zipping across his screen. "A German Humanist just invented the printing press! Means computers aren't far behind. It'll be tough to control those humanoids once they get computers. Things could go haywire fast. And we'll end up tossing that whole galaxy into the trash."

"I'd suggest we use a full Noahic intervention again. Make them start from scratch."

"I don't think so. I don't want to waste another couple-million years. Now that we have religion set in place, we should be able to use it. Jesus's church structure still embodies formidable anti-intellectual force. I'd like to try one of my anti-humanist-pope models. It should do the trick, and if we need enhancement, I can always send in the Spanish Inquisition. I'm betting in a couple hundred years those humanoids will be back crawling around in the stone age, and our experiment will again be on track."

"There, I just sent Pope Callixtus III in to do his work." Guilda says. "Science should be buried for another thousand years. I think we've time for a cigarette break. When we get back, it's possible the humanoid organism will've covered the globe and be ready to produce a harvestable blossom or two."

* * *

In the Cathedral in Lisbon, Portugal, on the day of the 1458 summer solstice, Pope Callixtus III, who arranged this event, calls Prince Henry, the Portuguese wunderkind, to his side and begins to speak to the assembled crowd:

"My Dear Children in Christ," the pope says, "we have come to a time of extreme importance in the battle between good and evil. I know that many of you have dedicated yourselves to reinvigorating the study of ancient Roman physics, astronomy and other so-called sciences. But studying such things has a horrible cost. Scientific studies are the work of the devil and undermine the teachings of Augustine, Aquinas and even Aristotle." He picks up a copy of the Papal Bull he's had composed for this occasion, and reads from it. "Our battle with the Great Satan is of paramount importance. Therefore, from this day, all study of science will be outlawed. Every book on science or humanism will be burned. We must rid ourselves of Roman science and continue a strong force against new Islamic science. And, secondly, we must convert the unknown parts of the world to Christ, so that Islamic science cannot take hold there either."

He turns to Henry of Portugal: "I'm ordering *my dearly beloved son*, Henry of Aviz and Governor of the Order of Christ in Portugal, to wage Crusade upon all of Africa and all other lands he may find, kill all unbelievers living there, and then bring those lands under the ecclesiastical jurisdiction of my Church."

A hundred dirty, armed, and incontinent Spanish Inquisition soldiers lurch down the side aisles and station themselves to the sides of the pope.

"My dear friends," Callixtus says, "I intend now to put fear into your hearts. From this point on, no so-called 'scientific' study will be allowed in all of Western Europe. I'm authorizing my *Holy*

Inquisition," he points a well-manicured pink finger toward the armed miscreants, "to enforce this prohibition against any man or nation who would study science in defiance of this Bull, or interferes with Henry's monopoly regarding his Crusading. All scientific books and humanist tracts must be turned over to the Holy Inquisition. And, just so you know, as I am speaking to you, my agents are stomping through your offices, libraries, and sleeping chambers, collecting and then burning your filthy science books."

"But your Excellency," pleads Henry, "my navigators need the mathematics and science to wage Holy Crusade in Africa and other unknown lands."

"Okay, fine! However, you must keep all your science a secret from your king and even from your friends in this room. You are ordered to burn or drown any man, even a king, who pilfers such dangerous information. Humanism must be excised from our universities, along with Islamic numbers and Ptolemy's Maps. The path to Hell is paved with humanist philosophy and science. It's all anti-Catholic nonsense."

Callixtus intends to force Henry to use his stature as the premier humanist and scientist of his time, to be his agent to crush humanist thinking. Henry and his organization will keep all scientific investigations secret, so that during the next several centuries, until well after Newton, no humanist-generated scientific information regarding the *actual* physical reality of the earth, sun and cosmos will be openly discussed anywhere in Western Europe.

"There! That should get the job done for another couple millennia," says Guilda.

* * *

However, when Guilda and Ross return from their coffee break they find their pretty blue planet has plunged itself into chaos. A virulent science and technology culture has developed while they were gone.

"I can't believe it," says Guilda. "We left them alone for only a few minutes and look at them! They're tampering with human genomes, storing information in cyber-clouds, even sending probes to other planets. What's happened to your Inquisition guys? They usually work efficiently. It's too late now, isn't it Ross? The machines are taking over here. The crazies really did it this time!"

"Remember—"

"Yeah, I know. Time does not exist! You keep telling me that, but they haven't much time left, do they?" asks Guilda. "I see science overpowering this humanoid culture. We should just let them crash and then start over on a new planet. We cut our losses, make the best use of our time."

"Patience, Guilda. Let's try one more intervention. I know just the thing to do the trick. I'll show you the power of a retro-religious intervention."

"What the hell is that?"

"If you thought the Spanish Inquisition was fun to watch, you'll love this. It's a new anti-rational device I've been developing."

"What's anti-rational mean?"

"Means machines have no power over it. It's like the *Spanish Inquisition*, but on steroids. I call it the *Banū 'Umayya Intervention* (BUI.) Back in the seventh and eighth centuries these sons of Umayya bloodied their swords from India to Gibraltar. I developed the BUI specifically for high-level technical conditions like this. I think it has the potential to drop humanoid society back into the fifth century. With both the BUI and the Incontinent Spanish Inquisition Soldiers (ISIS) destroying western civilization, no machine-infected culture will have the chance to develop the mechanical ability to stop the anti-technical plague."

"What? Did you just say machines can't efficiently kill people, only people can efficiently kill people?"

"Exactly! And the great part is that those hordes of rampaging anti-scientific sadists are designed specifically to excite the several Doomsday Christian cults who then immediately raise their own armies of anti-scientific zealots. Soon billions of crazy religious zealots on both sides will be screaming "jihad" or "crusade" and, in no time, all the reasonably educated humanoids and their machines on both sides will be destroyed. That will make everything ready for the spectacular finale. The great armies of the various Gods will slaughter each other one-on-one with swords and bludgeons. It'll be beautiful! We use Armageddon to advantage, just like my sign says." He points to the colorful mobile swaying gently above his desk.

"You're crazy," says Guilda. "What possible benefit is Armageddon? It won't work. That little planet is in the grip of an advanced and aggressive science infestation. Crazy guys, even lots of crazy guys, swinging swords and clubs can't overpower *science*. I'm thinking only Noahic floods or asteroid attacks can help us now."

"Oh ye of little faith," says Ross. "Ya got to be patient, Guilda. Eventually both sides see the inevitable good answer. First thing they'll do is work together to kill the machines—and that can easily be done because mass destruction devices are no good against masses of humanoids—they work only against specific targets in limited areas. The crazed masses will quickly realize that mass mechanical weapons cannot kill enough people, only huge uncoordinated masses of rabid people can kill the billions of uncoordinated masses of rabid people who need killing. And then the second truth: when masses of people are killing masses of people, the winner is not the side that kills the most people, but the side that produces the most people *to do the killing*."

"That makes absolutely no sense! What do you mean?"

"We know from computer models that when pushed to frenzied procreation, people can produce people faster than the people thus produced can be killed. In fact, they can't kill enough people to even feed the frenzied procreators. And that means soon the solid surface of the planet is stuffed full with humanoids."

"That's absolute nonsense, Ross. This entire experiment has gone off the rails. I can't help it, I need another cigarette."

"You keep smoking at that rate, it's gonna kill you, Guilda."

"No, it won't Ross. I ain't ever gonna die. Our work here will soon produce a DNA strain that will prevent all disease, even environmental disease like nicotine-lung. Once that serum comes on line, bingo! I ain't never gonna die."

"It's a fact, Guilda, that the entire energy of all humanoid cultures will create such breeding frenzies on both sides that the mass of humanoid sexual reproductive activity jumps the organism into producing…" Ross pushes a few keys and makes a deft move with three fingers on the touchscreen. "Taa daa! There's your flower burst. You can do the honors and harvest it. After that you can go smoke your cigarette."

Many natural organisms metamorphose into a form completely different in shape and nature than the original fungal stage, and humanoid fungal development is no different. Once masses of humanoids are forced to survive in dense clusters and feed on each other, such clusters will, under prolonged periods of hot sunlight and heavy rains, undergo metamorphoses. That results in the mass of humanoids producing the flowering non-humanoid thing Ross calls a *bloom*.

"It is that bloom of the fully metamorphosed human fungi that is the valuable commodity, Guilda. It's stuffed full of unadulterated human DNA. That is what we must harvest and preserve to ensure *our own future*.

"And the sad thing is that right now, hard workers like you and I do not have a future. When we die, we're dead. We have no future because when time doesn't exist, no future is possible."

And although everyone knows that time does not exist, there is this theory, the EHC (The Einstein-Hawking Conjecture), which contends that time, although non-existing, can still be experienced, as if it were real, under certain unique circumstances. There is, however, one big hurdle: any such experience must, of necessity, take place in the future. And, since time does not exist, it is difficult to understand how humans will be able to access this *future*. That's the problem that consumes Guilda and Ross. They're working on the assumption that the act of *humanoid fungi metamorphoses*, even at a microscopic level, is an act that allows an individual to access a dimension other than space or time.

"I'm hoping," says Ross, "that the metamorphic experience can jump across time and space barriers and access the conceptual reality that exists in this room. I'm hoping a colony of intellectuals injected with a serum made from the DNA of post-metamorphic microscopic humanoids will be able to overcome the handicap of living in the Einstein-Hawking Conjecture, a warped four-dimensional world where space and time are limited functions. The hope is that King Claudius can find the answer, a comforting place in space-time where an extra dimension or two will allow at least the concept of a future to exist."

"You realize, Ross, my future must be accessible *right now*. I want to be free now! I need that extra dimension."

"You're lucky, Guilda," says Ross. "You've got more time than I do to get to the future. I doubt there's enough time for Claudius's metamorphic enhancements to be integrated into my body. You, Guilda, have more time for the injection procedures to be finalized. I'm afraid I'm going to run out of time."

"You certainly are," she says. "And pretty damn soon, too! Remember, you jerk, '*Time does not exist!*' Therefore, you can never run out of it." Guilda gets up. "Speaking of time, Ross; It's now *Show Time*." She runs over to the exterior door, releases the time-latch, and swings the door in on its hinges.

The heavy metal door bursts full open with thunderous noise, slamming hard against the masonry wall. A dozen filthy ogres wearing colorful silk garments and wielding bludgeons burst into the room.

Guilda forces herself against the wall, out of the rush of smelly bodies. "Taa daa," she yells.

Ross jumps up from his chair. "Oh, God!" he yells. "I didn't expect the Spanish Inquisition!" He pushes a red button to generate the facility-wide alarm.

"But I did," she says. "Yippee! He's right on time." She runs over, throws her arms around the Strange Prince and gives him a passionate kiss.

"What's happening, Guilda? You're with ISIS?"

"You taught me all I know, Ross. *Machines are evil things*. You've spent your whole life smashing machines. Now it's my turn.

I will destroy this lab. It also is an evil machine. It too must be smashed. You, yourself, say it all the time: '*Kill the Machines.*'"

"But you can't kill *this* machine, you stupid twit!" He frantically jams the alarm button. "Don't you get it? If your Strange Prince and his Spanish Inquisition kill *this* machine, it means you *will* die! Unless I continue to kill ancient machines from this modern lab, your *future does not exist.*"

Guilda squeals with delight as one of her Strange Prince's ogres smashes his purple-stained bludgeon into the monitor of her machine. Black plastic shards hammer about the room. The smell is pungent, acrid, and a bit spicy.

"You're a fool, Guilda. If you kill these machines, your future vanishes and your retirement is toast! You'll run out of time."

"And who's gonna care, dearest Ross? As you constantly tell me, '*Time does not exist.*'"

"My future exists *right now*," says the Strange Prince, "but yours is *over*!" He may be an idiot, but he's physically quick, and with one swift pass of his rusty blade he severs Ross's noggin from its frame. The thing splats onto the concrete, rolls jerkily while flinging messy bits of DNA, and comes to rest against a waste receptacle directly under Ross's colorful sign.

The Strange Prince points his dripping blade at the sign. "*Instantaneous Armageddon!*"

"Oh my God," says Ross's head. That's all the thing could get out of his mouth.

Sprawled

David Culberson

Kevin rode in the passenger seat of the Global Bank Corp van, staring at the corporate computer pad in his lap. A bump caused him to glance up at oncoming traffic and the congestion on either side of the road. A Global Bank Corp sign caught his attention. Kevin looked down at his dark-gray collared shirt. It had patches on both shoulders that read *Global Bank Corp Animal Control and Park Maintenance* in bright red letters—the same red lettering that stamped almost everything Kevin knew.

"I remember my first day on the job," Sam, the wiry driver Kevin had met for the first time earlier that morning, said. "Things were sure different then. Mostly animal control. Now, they got us all learnin' about these damn computers and robotics and sheeit. 'Course, there was some crazy-ass animals back then. They got even crazier by the time we got rid of 'em—most of 'em anyways."

Kevin didn't want to talk. He looked out at the passing scenery—hills and valleys covered with gated residential communities made up of one- and two-story zero-lot line homes interrupted by two- or three-story strip malls and commercial centers—the same landscape of roofs, walls, roads and signs that formed the backdrop of his entire life. Few trees could be seen, a single oak here, a small copse there. He'd seen forests only a few times in his life. When he was younger, his parents had taken him to several Global Bank Corp parks. "So you'll understand nature, son," they'd told him, though what they called *nature* seemed a bit off to him. It looked to him like things made to look real, but he couldn't be sure since it was all he knew.

Sam looked at Kevin and said, "You're lookin' nervous, Kid. You nervous?"

Kevin's eyes darted to his computer pad, which he had yet to turn on. The pad had been part of his training the past six weeks. It helped him memorize a detailed map of the park he was to help maintain, identify animal and plant species, and learn genetic mutation sequences. It also supported his weapons training and hands-on knowledge of the glorified first aid kit in the back of the van. He *was* nervous. Training was over and he was about to see the real world as he'd never seen it.

He offered a weak smile. "I'm okay."

"You got nothin' to worry about. This job's easy as pie. Sheeit, you'll do fine. You got me to show you the ropes. Ain't nobody better," Sam said and laughed.

This wasn't Kevin's dream job. He would have preferred to write, but his term papers in high school drew the attention of Global Bank Corp's security offices and, when his controversial ideas continued through his college reports and Internet blog, the mega-corporation shut him down. They had him booted from college but, through his parents' contacts, he was able to enroll in Global Bank Corp Maintenance Training, where he found the classes filled mostly with underachieving ex-students and has-been corporate middle managers. Kevin laughed to himself after the first full day of class. When he was young, he and his friends called out, "*Robot herders*," to the vans with red letters each time one drove by. The phrase came from the constant rumors about the park's unusually tame wildlife being under the control of the people in the white vans. Now he was one of them.

Kevin thought about Sam's words and said, "I thought we were called out to find a big cat."

"We were, along with some routine maintenance of herds and trees. Fuckin' tourists are always screwin' with trees, tryin' to take pieces of 'em out of the park to prove they ain't real. You'd think they'd learn after a few electric shocks to stop screwin' with 'em," Sam said with a smile.

Kevin putzed with his computer pad, trying not to look as nervous as he felt.

Sam leaned over and said, "Don't worry, Kid. They ain't no big cats around anymore—none we can't control, anyways."

"But, in school I heard about weird animals that roam the parks. I heard that they've killed people. That they're mutants because the parks are so landlocked that the animals had to inbreed—those that didn't go extinct. I heard that Global is hiding it."

"That's a bunch of liberal gobbledygook. Where'd you learn that crap? School? Or are you one of those Internet junkies that thinks Global is evil? That makin' a profit is bad?"

How much profit are we making? Kevin thought, not daring to ask and risk being called a smart ass—for the umpteenth time in his life—and especially by his new boss.

"I just heard it, that's all," Kevin said and looked out the window. Then he turned to Sam and said, "And more than once."

"Sheeit, Kid. Global is our boss. They're everybody's boss. Except for those still workin' in what's left of the government, that is." Sam looked at Kevin and said, "You'd better straighten your attitude out—unless you wanna be one of those government weenies. Talk about worthless." Sam snorted and continued to drive.

After a few miles he said, "Global succeeded. Others didn't. Disney tried. They sucked at it." He cocked his head and pointed to a small valley in the distance below the passenger side of the van. "See those mustard-colored roofs and walls?"

Kevin squinted as he scanned the valley.

"The ones in the middle. See? They're the old ones. Some of the first ones built, back when Disney contracted with the government after the war to start the housing campaign. You know what they say: 'housing and war, the only consistent economic stimuli throughout history.' 'Course, that was before high-tech. But once we installed that Star Wars defense sheeit, wars was over. Now it's housing and high-tech. And the government pushed the hell out of both. All the rich defense contractors with political contacts scrambled into real estate and park management. Disney dominated the market first with all their fake-lookin' sheeit. Then Global got the contract. Their sheeit doesn't look so fake. Rumor is that Global had control of the government by then and forced Disney out."

Kevin looked back at the mustard-colored mass of buildings in the middle of thousands of other, newer rooftops, wondering if this was just some bullshit Sam had made up. Not that any of it mattered.

Sam continued, "Global owns those old Disney communities now. That's where they let the poor people buy homes—there and in the center of the cities, a long way from here."

"How did Global force Disney out?" Kevin asked, not really interested but thinking that he needed to sound so—his first day and all.

"That's a good question, Kid. The Supreme Court passed a law a couple decades ago, around the year 2005 I think, that allowed any private company to ask the government to condemn property for the better economic good of the community. I don't think the government knew what hit 'em by the time Global was done. They had all the Disney properties. Hell, they had all their competition's properties condemned when they showed up in courts with new community financial models and the cash to back it up. They even took over all the state parks and developed them into gated communities and sheeit. They've taken over all the federal parks east of the Mississippi and put houses and schools and strip malls around them. They claim land near the parks is more valuable, since there ain't much park left anymore." Sam laughed and added, "Pretty fuckin' smart if you ask me."

Kevin fiddled with his computer, occasionally looking out at the rooftops.

Sam said, "It was a stroke of genius for Global to have property condemned for the economic good of Global. That's why we got jobs, Kid. Don't you get it?"

Kevin smiled but said nothing. After a long pause, Sam said, "You still worried about rogue, mutant animals?"

Kevin shrugged.

"Well, Kid, it's bullsheeit. I've had to kill a few animals in the past. And I've seen some lone critters runnin' through the forest, but I'm pretty sure that they're just some of ours that got their wires crossed. They'll quit runnin' eventually. Can't live without us," Sam said and slowed the van. He pointed out a narrow road to the right. "There's our turn."

Sam turned onto the road and within a few hundred feet made a sharp right turn onto a gravel road. "Besides, any animal we come across not in our control has to be killed. It's corporate rules." Sam nodded toward the back of the van. "And we got plenty of weapons to get the job done if we see any."

Sam stopped the van and said, "Time to earn our money." He started to set up the map and GPS locator on the dashboard.

Kevin looked out the window to the small valley below. His jaw dropped. He'd never seen so many trees. And there were no buildings. It was different than the tourist part of the park he'd seen as a child.

"Quite a sight, ain't it, Kid? I remember the first time I saw it. 'Course, there was still some forests left here and there back then, so it wasn't all that unusual to see this," Sam said with a nod to the forest, then went back to the controls.

Kevin offered a weak smile and continued to scan the forest. *Maybe this job's not so bad,* he thought. The vegetation was thick close to the van but halfway down the slope to the valley was a clearing with only tall grass. On the other side of the clearing were tall trees and a bushy undergrowth. It was a beautiful sight. He took a deep breath and relaxed—until he saw it. Fifty yards down the slope in the clearing. It was no animal he recognized—nothing he'd seen in the training manuals or in any book he'd looked through as a child. It was the size of a large dog but more feline-like, with abnormally large shoulders and mangy, brown fur. It had loped out of the undergrowth and into the clearing, where it stopped and looked toward the van. Its head was a mass of long, black fur. Its snout squashed onto its face and long whiskers shot out from either side of its nose. Its lower jaw hung slightly open, showing off a gnarly set of teeth that would have fit better into the jaws of a Mako shark, if Sam remembered correctly the photos of sharks he'd seen in books. But it was the eyes that shook him to the core. The large black pupils with red bloodshot rims looked directly at him, as if challenging him to follow. Then it disappeared back up the slope.

God, what was that, he thought. He gripped his pad.

"Did you see that?" Kevin asked.

"What?" Sam said and looked toward Kevin.

Kevin continued to stare out the window. How could he start to describe the hideous animal without his new boss laughing him out of the van?

"Ah, nothing."

"You look scared, Kid."

"No. I ju-just thought I saw something. Maybe a loose dog."

Sam turned the screen mounted on the dash toward Kevin and said, "Well, Kid. Look at the screen. All our animals are accounted for and there ain't nothin' within a quarter mile of us. No loose dog—nothin'. And there ain't supposed to be nothin', neither."

Kevin turned to look at the screen and shrugged. "Yeah. Must have been a shadow."

Sam put the van into drive and within a hundred yards they passed a sign that read *Shenandoah National Park – Property of Global Bank Corp, Employee Entrance.* A quarter mile later, Sam slowed at the top of a ridge. Below was a paved road that led to a parking lot used by tourists to take advantage of the panoramic view of a valley below and the herds of buffalo and elk that shared it. No elk were in sight but a herd of buffalo grazed about three hundred yards down the slope. Kevin knew that buffalo and elk shouldn't be found this far east but he'd learned in his job-training classes that Global displayed animals in their parks that tourists wanted to see, not necessarily what they would expect to find. He remembered joking with an acquaintance during class that Global should put elephants and tigers in their parks, and maybe a few orangutans, too.

Sam grinned. "Come on, Kid. Let's have some fun."

Sam parked the van out of view of the tourists. He got out and walked to the edge of the service road with his computer pad under his arm. Kevin followed. They stopped behind a large bush.

Sam laughed and said, "Watch this."

He turned his pad on and entered a series of passwords. Once he obtained security clearance he opened the screen to a map that showed their area in live time, including the movements of any human or animal within a quarter mile. He moved the cursor to the side of the screen and clicked. The buffalo herd the tourists were watching from behind a tall fence instantly stampeded in their direction.

Sam turned to Kevin and snorted. He said, "Look at the stupid tourists runnin' for their cars."

Kevin watched the tourists scramble. A few stragglers were caught with their smart phones pressed against their faces and couldn't see the big picture of five hundred buffaloes charging toward them. Some were jerked back by friends or family. Others froze when they lowered their smart phones and realized what was happening.

Sam's shoulders heaved up and down in cadence to his belly laughs. When the buffaloes were within fifty feet of the fence he clicked the cursor again and the herd stopped their charge as abruptly as they had started. Their heads lowered to the green carpet and they grazed as though nothing had happened. Some of the tourists drove away. Some lingered in the parking lot near their cars and watched the herd. Others frantically pushed buttons on their smart phones, undoubtedly reporting the stampede to authorities, who would call Sam and Kevin to investigate.

Kevin looked at Sam and said, "What if they didn't stop?"

"They had to. That's the way they're programmed. Didn't you learn that in trainin', Kid?"

Kevin started to walk back to the van.

"Hey, come on. I'm just fuckin' with the tourists. No big deal."

Sam turned off his computer and walked to the van. Once inside he looked at Kevin and said, "What? No sense of humor?"

Kevin looked out the window, still spooked by the animal he'd seen earlier. Sam started up the van and backed out onto the gravel road. "Sheeit. Kids these days," he said, more to himself than to Kevin.

Sam drove the van back toward the entrance and said, "Listen. We're gonna be workin' together for a long time. Every now and again we need to be havin' some fun. Otherwise the job's borin'."

Kevin shrugged but didn't respond. He knew they were heading back where they came from—toward the animal.

"Where you from, Kid?" Sam asked with a big smile as he turned down a different gravel road than the one they'd come in on.

"Where are we going?" Kevin asked.

"I'm hungry. You hungry, Kid?"

"Yeah, I am," Kevin said, glad to be going somewhere different than the entrance.

"There's a commissary for employees down the road a piece. They got good food. Thought we'd pick up a couple sandwiches and take 'em to this scenic overlook that's close by. It's not an official overlook. Just a picnic table and restroom for employees. But it's got a sheeit-kickin' view down the valley."

"That sounds good," Kevin said.

"So, Kid, where did you say you're from?"

"Akron. It's a suburb of Chicago."

"Yeah, I know the place." Sam paused for a while and said, "Did you know that Akron used to be a city in a state called Ohio?"

Kevin had studied history. He knew.

"Hell, Akron is close to where the suburbs of Chicago and New York City meet."

Sam drove up to a small block building. A few other Global vans were parked outside.

"This park used to be in a state called West Virginia. Now it's in the suburbs of Washington, DC. I remember when Global announced that they'd taken it over after the government condemned it—along with the rest of the national parks east of the Mississippi. That was only about sixteen years ago. You were probably too young to remember."

They got out of the van and walked toward the building. Sam continued, "I hear there are still a few states left out west. I mean, the coast is either Los Angeles or Seattle. But between us and them are some states without all this development. I think Montana and Idaho and maybe Wyoming are still states. I know there ain't many. Sheeit, Minneapolis just incorporated Denver as a suburb last year. Imagine that."

Sam ordered burgers, fries and drinks for both of them. They took their orders back to the van. Once inside Sam said, "Wait 'til you see the view where we're gonna eat."

Kevin looked at the bag of food and asked, "Where does this stuff come from? Who raises the beef and grows food? I've never seen a farm."

"Another good question, Kid. You're gonna be alright." Sam made a turn to the left. "Altanta has a bunch of factory farms in its eastern suburbs near the Atlantic Coast. Communities around them are cheap to buy into 'cuz the pigs and cattle stink. Global claims they've been workin' on some genetically altered feed for the pigs to take the smell out of their sheeit. But I hear it doesn't work so well."

Sam turned down a narrow dirt road. "Chicago has a bunch of corporate farms in its southern suburbs that grow grain and vegetables and sheeit. Most of it feeds beef and pigs though. The rest goes to make these fries," Sam said with a smile and poked the bag that sat on the floor between them. "They're pretty good, too."

Sam pulled the van onto a grassy knoll that overlooked a wide valley with steep slopes on either side. There were no houses or buildings in sight. Just trees. Even when his parents took him to see the parks, there had always been buildings on the edges of the park and Global maintenance offices close by. Sam and Kevin got out of the van and walked to a picnic table near the edge of the knoll. Sam's phone rang. He answered it and after listening for a minute hung up.

"There's some fuckin' tourists tryin' to climb some trees near where we left the buffaloes. You stay here. I'll go shoo 'em away. Maybe I'll turn the juice on to shock them a little. Watch 'em drop out of the trees like dead bugs. That'll be fun. Depends how high up they are, though. Don't want 'em to get hurt," Sam said with a laugh. He grabbed one of the burgers and some fries from the bag and walked back to the van. He backed it out onto the narrow road and hollered out the window, "I'll be back in a few minutes. Enjoy the view, Kid."

Kevin smiled and took a bite of his burger. It was good. He reached into the bag and grabbed a handful of fries. They were good, too. He chewed and watched the valley below. His spirits rose. Maybe the horrible animal he'd seen earlier was a shadow or his imagination. He pulled out another few fries and turned to look at the forest behind him. A squirrel bounded down a small tree and scampered toward the picnic table, stopping and sitting upright on its haunches a few feet away.

Was it real, Kevin wondered? He'd left his computer pad in the van and had no way of knowing if it was a Global animal without a computer scan—unless he shot it and there was blood. But he didn't have a weapon, and the squirrel seemed friendly. He felt silly offering it a fry, but he did anyway. The squirrel bounced up to him and took the fry. It backed up a few feet, sat on its haunches and used its small front feet to hold the fry while it nibbled around the edges.

"I'll be damned," Kevin said out loud. "It's fucking real."

Kevin reached for another fry when three baby squirrels cautiously came out of the bush and scampered to the larger squirrel. "You're their mother, aren't you?" Kevin said to the squirrel. "Wait until Sam sees this."

Kevin reached down toward the baby squirrels and held out another fry. Two of them held back, chirping at their mother. One came forward and, as it closed the distance between it and the fry, Kevin saw that its head was unusually large for its body and it had a menacing-looking face, different than that of its mother. Kevin wasn't deterred. How often, if ever, had he seen a real animal? And now he was feeding them.

The baby squirrel reached the fry but, instead of taking it, bit Kevin's finger.

Kevin dropped the fry with a loud, "Ouch. Shit. That hurt."

The mother squirrel chirped and the baby returned to her side without the fry. Kevin started to offer the mother a piece of hamburger bun when he heard an ear-piercing high-pitched screech behind him. The mother squirrel ran back to the trees. The babies followed. Kevin turned to see the monster cat with the large head and gnarly teeth running in his direction. Kevin had no weapon and he couldn't run even if he had a place to hide. He was frozen in his seat. The cat continued toward him, veering off the last few feet when it spotted the last of the baby squirrels trying to escape into the forest. It pounced on the squirrel and ate it in one gulp.

Kevin stood and moved toward the edge of the knoll. Maybe there was a cliff he could jump down. The cat turned and stared at Kevin, its red-rimmed black eyes looking for the next meal, and Kevin knew he was it. He backed away. Jumping off a cliff, if one existed on the edge of the knoll, would be a better way to go, he thought.

The cat sprang. A shot rang out. Kevin hit the ground, having no idea what was going on. He heard the cat fall a few feet from him. Beyond the cat's supine body, at the edge of the forest, he saw the mother squirrel and her two remaining babies peering back toward him. He heard the sound of footsteps coming closer. The mother squirrel looked above and behind him to whatever was making the footfalls.

"Sheeit, Kid. What the fuck did you get yourself into? Jesus, I leave you for a few minutes and you attract this monster?" Sam said. He walked to the cat and poked it with the barrel of his rifle.

Kevin stood up and brushed the dirt from his pants. His armpits were soaked with sweat.

Sam pulled his rifle to his shoulder and put a bullet into the cat's head. "Just need to make sure," he said and walked over to Kevin. "You alright, Kid?"

Kevin pointed to the cat and said, "Is that thing real?"

"You didn't see sparks come out, did you?" He pointed to the pool of blood beneath the cat's body and said, "That's blood. It's real. Who'd make a robot like this, anyways? It'd scare the sheeit out of the tourists. You'd better check your pants, Kid. Maybe it scared the sheeit out of you," Sam said with a laugh.

"I'm alright," Kevin said and started to gather up the spilled food on the ground.

"Forget that for now, Kid. Help me get this beast into the van. There's a big canvas tarp in the back. We'll roll it up and take it to Animal Disposal."

"You told me there weren't any of these things in the park," Kevin said.

"Well, I lied. They ain't many. And I didn't expect you to run into one, not your first day, anyways."

They struggled with the heavy cat and got it into the back of the van. Kevin turned to pick up the food and bag from around the picnic table. The mother squirrel had come out of the forest and was gnawing at the burger. Her two remaining babies were taking turns on a fry.

Kevin walked up to them and said to Sam, who was coming out of the van, "Watch this." He bent down with a fry in his hand and held it out to the mother. She took it and chirped at her babies.

Sam walked up behind him. "Kid, those are real."

"I know. Just like the cat. But these squirrels are nice. The mother is, anyway."

Sam said, "They need to be killed. You know that, right?"

"But there's nothing wrong with them."

Sam walked closer to the squirrels. "Look at the babies. They're deformed. Their heads are too big." For the first time Sam noticed blood coming from Kevin's finger. "Did one of these bite you?"

"One of the babies. But it was my fault. I got too close."

"It's aggressive, but the mother ain't. Kid, maybe the mother's fine but these babies have mutated."

"But I can take care of them. At least I can try to save the mother."

"She won't last, Kid. And if she does, she'll breed with mutant male squirrels. Sheeit, she already has." Sam pointed to one of the babies that had bounced a foot toward Sam and sat on its haunches chirping, its menacing eyes darting from Sam to Kevin.

"But…"

"Come on, Kid. You trained for this. They have to be destroyed."

"But I could take the mother to one of the states out west and let her go where there are still wildlife corridors and maybe other healthy animals."

Sam raised his rifle. "Go back to the van, Kid. I'll do this."

"But, Sam, you can't get them all. As soon as you shoot one the others will run."

"No they won't. I'll shoot the mother first. The young ones will stay around long enough for me to kill 'em. They might even attack. Look at their eyes."

"But…"

"Go, Kid. It's our job. 'For the greater good.' You learned that the first day of training."

Kevin walked to the van and stepped up into the passenger seat. He looked back at the canvas bag that covered the big cat—the cat that had almost killed him. He turned to look out over the valley. Such a pretty place. He heard the shots—bang, then bang, bang. He continued to stare into the valley when Sam came back to the van and opened the side door. He placed the rifle back into its bracket against the inside of the van and grabbed a canvas bag. A minute later he was back and gently placed the bloodied bag next to the body of the cat, then slid the door shut.

When Sam was back in the driver's seat, he said, "You alright, Kid?"

Kevin took a last look at the valley and imagined what it would have been like to have lived with real animals—not inbred mutants or the robotic animals he was charged with maintaining. He couldn't.

Sam's phone rang. He answered and after a few seconds said they'd be right there.

"A couple of elk have gone and toppled over. They're like sore thumbs in the middle of the herd, on their sides with their legs sprawled out in front of 'em and kickin' in the wind, like they're runnin' or somethin'. We need to stand 'em back up before more tourists scream their heads off. Like we're mistreatin' the animals. Fuckin' tourists."

Kevin laughed and said, "Let's go get 'em, boss."

American Skin

Ian Graham Leask

The small, high-altitude town had been wedged into a gulch during a gold rush and now the mountains were taking it back. The astronaut had seen it from orbit, found out all there was to know about it, and now looked for the store on Main Street where he had agreed to meet Mrs. Bjornsen at noon. Several abandoned buildings had saplings gnarling through them. Rusting American-made trucks were parked on the streets, and he wondered how the locals would feel about his electric 4X4; it shouted *here comes a rich motherfucker*. He felt strange being in the town after dreaming about it from out there—this fuzzy smudge on Earth's surface that he had chosen— sometimes you had to travel to a fuzzy smudge, and, as you got closer, its details came into focus and you got used to it.

The steep street curved and opened up into a condensed area constellating a bank, a small supermarket, a cafe, a sports shop and a souvenir store. He parked outside the souvenir store like the other vehicles—head-on to the curb—and locked his truck with the electronic key. A withered brown man in a red ball cap, sitting on a bench outside the left plate-glass window of the store, with what looked like a wolf splayed at his feet, reacted to the sound of the locking mechanism by sneering at him. He nodded at the man but avoided eye contact. A bell rang as he entered and a woman wearing a straw cowboy hat stood up behind a glass counter and smiled.

The woman did not have blue hair as he had expected. Her hair was long and blonde, a little too young for her, and she wore all denim—shirt and jeans. Up closer he noticed her white teeth contrasted too much with her tanned face. Before he went to Space he had called this the Denver look—the mindless destruction of skin cells through sun tanning; such things no longer bothered him.

The other window—not the one with the old man's plaid-shirted back against it—was full of dream-catchers, and the store smelled of new leather and potpourri. He looked at the boxes full of trinkets opened on the floor. "You must be Jonah," said the woman, and came out from behind the counter, holding out her hand. "I'm Karin." Her hand felt warm and a little calloused. He stared at her hand too long, trying to get it under control. He liked that she didn't acknowledge his celebrity. She was nearly his height and her touch sent a pulse through him, which was odd because he could not have said at first that she was particularly attractive. "I'm not always ripped apart like this," she said. "I'm getting ready for winter season. Not that there's likely to be one."

Stupidly, he said, "I'm here for the cabin."

What an idiot—Space-brain.

He felt shamed by the look she gave him—like he had insulted her friendliness. "Okay, then," she said, shrugging. "Let's go look at it."

* * *

She drove a big dented green truck that had once been owned by the forest service. The tarmac ended fifty meters before the house and the dirt road wound up the mountain past the house and into the forest. Through the cut in the road the sight of a gray-blue granite peak with snow on it made his heart beat faster. He had zeroed in on this mountain from the orbiter in the weeks before returning and now it was bigger than him, much bigger. It was part of the skin of the world, just like his skin under a microscope, tragically uneven with ridges and valleys, blotches, and for some reason he could not identify, he felt spooked. Fuck this, he thought, what's wrong with me? Maybe this place isn't suitable, after all. He recalled the counselors warning that his instincts might be out of whack for a while. Relax, he told himself. Settle in like a human.

Rust fell through the inside of the truck's door when he slammed it. They stood side-by-side, looking at the mountain. Karin's coat smelled of gasoline but her hair smelled of shampoo. There was also the smell of pinesap and the treated logs of the house. He looked at the house. He had seen its roof from Space but had not imagined it was alive like this. She must have caught reticence in his face because she started right up with the discounts and guilt trips, and although he didn't fall for them, he agreed to rent the place once he saw the inside. He wasn't sure why because the whole situation frightened him. Neither did he know why it frightened him. He understood that the fear came from inside him, not from the place itself, and that it was a fear created by seeing things others had not seen, but knowing that did not help him understand this particular fear. And then there was Karin. The moment she set eyes on him she displayed availability. He wanted to work, to write the memoir, and not enter into fresh complications. He tried to hint at this by having Karin help him pull a table under the window so he could work while looking at the mountain.

Hinting did not seem to work since she became giddy when she showed him the master bedroom with its gigantic bed built of local timber. He knew what was in her mind. He asked to look at the appliances. The place smelled fresh and there was no dust. The appliances looked functional. The space was minimalist, a little too big, but he would get used to that; you can get used to anything.

"It's very nice," he said. "Why don't you live here?"

She looked at her hands for a moment—no rings—a gesture he found peculiar—before saying, "Bad memories in here for me. And I have to mind the store."

Karin said she liked that he was going to sequester himself to try and write a book, so she gave him a break on the rent. She was clearly desperate to lease the place, but he realized that he was equally desperate to get started on the work. It felt like he had limited time even though there was no reason to believe that—he had checked out just fine. He liked that she didn't ask him what the book was about because he would struggle to explain it to her. He felt better suddenly. It was exactly what he needed; he must get over this strange haywire in his intuition. After all, what did it matter? He would give her the cold shoulder and she would leave him alone. He knew how to do it, to say no to indulgence, although he had not been good at saying no in the past. "I'll want a lot of privacy," he blurted. He was not sure what his face looked liked when he said this because she recovered well and said, "No worries, Jonah. You got it."

* * *

It took him nearly a month to formulate a plan for the book. A structure. It should not have been hard; he might have been better off just starting and letting the text go where it wanted. He was too in control, and that had been what caused the trouble in the first place—way too much time in a planned environment. He decided to keep the structure as a guideline and let the text grow organically.

This decision caused him writer's block and he did a lot of walking and running as the first snows came.

Karin brought him an organic fruitcake and a blueberry pie and a lot of frozen moose meat from the previous season. She had to keep checking the septic system. He sat on the porch with her; had beer and coffee out there with her—wrapped in Pueblo blankets—but they did not go in the house together. He knew she wanted him; he could smell it on her. She was alone in the town and the other tradespeople spoke well of her but would not say much about her. Sometimes she drove in her green truck up the mountain but left him alone. He wondered what she did up there.

One day she roared by and waved at him on her way down and he liked the look of her smile as she waved. It was a sort of defeated smile and he felt bad for her, so he followed her down in his truck to give her his rent check early. He found her in her shop. She seemed elated by the early check. He had cut what was left of his hair very short and she kept looking at him. He laughed and said, "What?" She blushed and said, "You've done something."

"Buzzed my hair."

"Now you look like that old singer—Sting."

"A graying Sting?"

She splayed her hand in the middle of his chest and pushed slightly, moving him backwards toward the counter. "When are you going to have a log fire up there and invite me for wine?"

"I thought the place had bad vibes for you."

"Fires, wine and famous astronauts might get me over the past."

"I'm working hard," he said, laughing. "No time for fires and frivolity."

Her eyes did a funny little jig and she said, "Who do you think I look like?"

"You look like you."

"Not one for dancing, are you? Come on, play."

With as much charm as he could muster, he said, "I guess you look a bit like Sting too, but the female genotype. A lot of us look like that—generic white."

"Damn those Vikings."

He laughed at her and felt sorry that he would not invite her up for wine. She put her hand, open, on him again, this time sans any push, and he felt sadness rising. She said, "You got a lot of crap going on, don't you, hon. But I can feel a lovely heart in there, like a strong spring breeze."

He laughed bitterly and said, "No, Mrs. Bjornsen, this old heart's more like a hand grenade."

Karin laughed, stood away from him and said, "You and me— unexploded ordnance. I hate to think what the fuck you're writing up there."

She sent him home with fresh venison sausage loosely wrapped in paper. He left it on the porch swing to freeze. His Space-brain made him forget it and it sat there for days.

The writing started to come, but after a few sessions he found himself upset and depressed. The work went well though and he knew that to sustain it he needed to be outside in the light and not stay too long brooding at his desk. He didn't want what he wrote, but he had to write it because it was true. Nothing had ever been written about Space that was truly true; he had been raised with beautiful lies and the world would be less colorful without them. Four years of orbiting around planets had taught him the truth about how things are made, and living so precariously—and surviving—had taught him to overcome fear, but without fear you were vulnerable.

He would rise early, run hard up the plowed road, and then return for coffee and toast. He would work till late afternoon, make food, eat it, and go out for a walk up the mountain road, or use snowshoes to wander the woods. One day, while snowshoeing, he thought he heard a bear snorting. When he got home he noticed the venison sausage was gone and the snow around the porch looked disturbed. He rang Karin.

She was quiet, which worried him, and then she said, "They should be hibernating by now, Jonah. But you never know with bears. They do what they like."

"Should I be worried?"

"Just don't be waving succulent food around. Be smart."

"Okay. Asteroid showers are one thing, bears are another."

"They're misunderstood—just like the rest of us."

That night he listened for a bear moving around the cabin, but it was a night of extraordinary silence. He tried not to fall asleep so he could listen to the silence. No sound at all, not even the building settling, not even tree branches cracking in the cold; no wind rushing past. He could feel the mountain's presence in the silence and he could smell his own skin. He would write in the morning and the writing would have bear underneath it but no bear would be mentioned. He dreamed of silence and when he woke he realized that he had never dreamed of silence before and that it was not just a dream, but a nightmare.

He started work before his run—so that he could get the images onto the screen. Often, he forgot important things, or at least things that seemed important. As he wrote he remembered the litany of things that had injured him and how he had never shown any hurt to anyone. Because of this they thought he was very strong, even aloof. He became emotional and decided to get it under control by running up the mountain road in the morning sunshine. He put on his running gear and took off.

He ran all the way up the mountain road to where it terminated at a small abandoned quarry. Or perhaps it was a gold mine, he wasn't sure. There had once been some kind of building there, which was now just ruined half-walls obscured by snowdrifts. Someone from town plowed the road all the way to the top. He had never been up so far and running hard at this altitude made him dizzy; his vision tunneled so that he noticed tire marks in the turnabout. Breathing heavily, he looked out over the treetops to the other mountains and the plain that he had come from weeks ago. He felt happy. Loudly, he spoke to the open space:

"I'm not young anymore, but I am in one piece. I'm okay. I can run up a mountain. What is there left to fear?" His words sounded trite but he didn't care, provided they were true. Would they be true later tonight? Yes, he was okay. He started running down the mountain road and noticed that going down hurt his knees. The irony made him laugh—harder downhill than up. He ran mindlessly for a while, going slowly, with heavy footfalls on the icy slopes. A couple times he nearly fell. He could smell rancid sweat on his running jacket, which he had not bothered to launder since he arrived. He ran into denser woods and loved the fresh snow on everything and how the pines held the snow like cake icing. His breath steamed out ahead of him and the tight world of white woods closed in about him.

And then he heard the bear. He looked around behind him and saw it flying out of the trees at him. It flew two meters off the ground. He ran. He heard it land and looked back again to see its brownish black bulk lumbering after him, its paws solidly striking the ground. "What's happening?" He shouted, but kept running. A pulse of electric numbness shot down his spine to his legs, making them feel leaden, as if magic was helping the animal find its food. The message in his brain, not a verbal one but something akin to the discovery of God, told him to run like hell, and he felt the wind flying past him as age and time and history disappeared and there was only the snorting bear and the engine of his body, attempting to outrun a predator.

But you can't outrun a bear.

He knew the road turned sharply ten meters ahead, and sank downward. He could hug it tightly, avoiding the ice, while the bear might slide. He executed this plan with no pride or acknowledgment that once he would have panicked and screamed. He reached the corner and slowed himself on a moss-encrusted boulder. The bear, which was closer than he realized, indeed rushed onto the ice and skidded across the road and down the slope into the ditch. It passed him within inches, huge and heavy like a horse, and smelling like zoo. It swung around as it slid and looked directly into his eyes with no shame and no anger, only the confusion of being out of control; but its eyes were locked on his: *You're not getting away, meat.*

He started back up the hill, sprinting against the elevation, looking for an outlet, a weapon, a cabin. Within seconds his heart was bursting with the multiplied effort and his vision went pink. He felt sharp pain in his chest. At the next turn in the road he looked and the bear ran close behind him, all its fur jumping with effort. You're dead. Will this hurt? Be smart—try the same trick again. He saw another patch of ice, avoided it, spun around it, and attempted to burst past the bear, but it threw out a claw and sent him tumbling down the hill. Even as he tumbled he saw the bear slide again on the ice, and he wanted to insult it, call it an idiot. No wonder you're still a bear! He got up and ran with blood half-blinding him. He wondered if he had any face left.

His plan was to make the boulder again, but he doubted the bear could be fooled the same way. He looked for a variation but he could feel the bear very close, radar, like when you feel protruding objects in the dark. What a waste of these extraordinary senses—to just be slaughtered for food.

Around the corner came the front of a green truck.

The horn blared. He ran toward it. The truck came right at him and he understood that he must jump sideways into the snow-drifted ditch. He did this and together with the rush and slither of the snow-filled ditch, heard the truck smack into the bear. He heard an oomph from the bear and a thud and breaking glass, but then he was upside down, struggling for breath in the snow. He scrambled in a panic. As he found light again, gasping for breath, he heard shots that almost burst his eardrums.

He stood up to his chest in the drift, looking into the road where Karin, walking forward with a large silver gun in both hands, fired repeatedly into the retreating bear. The gun jumped upwards in her hands with each shot and he smelled the cordite of the shells. The bear stopped and lay down and she went right up to it and shot it through the eye. It steamed, but remained still. He could see no blood on it yet but his own blood kept seeping into his eyes.

He pulled himself out of the snow and climbed back into the road. He went to her and asked, "Are you okay?"

She looked at him seriously and he noticed for the first time the blue of her eyes. He felt dizzy. She took him by the arm and helped him across the ice to the cab of the truck, where she threw the big handgun onto the driver's seat and pulled a handful of pink Kleenex from a box on the passenger seat and pressed the wad against his forehead. The pressure made him see stars. Exhaust from the idling engine made him want to vomit.

"That thing was flying," he said.

"They certainly can move," she replied.

"No. It flew."

"How many fingers am I holding up?"

"Three."

"What day of the week is it?"

"Saturday?"

"You'll be okay. Lucky I like driving up to the old DNR compound."

"Lucky, indeed. Stalk me all you like from now on."

She laughed. "Oh, yes—you are so in my debt."

He laughed with her. Now there would have to be wine by the fire. Fine. He was alive. He said, "You were amazing."

"Yeah? Well, I'm going to be more amazing. You sit tight in here and I'm going to get that old pelt-bag into the flatbed. Keep these tissues tight to your noggin."

She strapped the seatbelt across him, handed him a half-bottle of water with a smear of lipstick on the rim, came around to the driver's side, and got in. The hood of the truck was turned up and crinkled, and the bear had flattened out in the road, already looking like a rug—maybe one with children hiding beneath it.

Karin drove uphill, a little beyond the dead bear, and then got out. Jonah realized he was concussed and couldn't concentrate on how she rigged up a pulley system in the nearest tree with yellow rope. He tried to turn and watch out the cab window but he ached all over and felt sick. He blanked out for a while, thinking nothing, and then was brought back by the bounce of the truck as a huge weight settled into it. Karin sat beside him in the cab. She had a rope wrapped in her leather gloves and had inched the load down from the Mountain Oak and into the flatbed. She must have trussed up the bear, thrown the rope over the tree and then driven uphill with the truck. Very clever. All he could say was, "We're going to have to let the DNR know about this, you understand?"

She said, "Ain't no DNR no more." And then she understood that he was joking and said, "You're a laugh a minute all of a sudden. You should get slugged by bears more often." She put a Pueblo blanket over him and said, "We're headed into town. Get a stitch on that gash. Keep that pink tissue tight. Makes you look awful pretty."

When he laughed, his ribs hurt. He felt ripped flesh under the pink tissues.

Karin parked the truck in back of the small supermarket where he bought his groceries. They went in together and found the old man who had been sitting outside her store on the day Jonah first arrived. After hearing the story the old man put a stitch in Jonah's forehead; his breath smelled of cigarettes and peppermint. His name was Frank Whitetree and he was the sheriff and store-owner and town medic, and most important of all, the butcher. "This is good fortune," he said, washing his hands. "Whole town gonna eat on that bear. Son of a bitch been raiding our garbage. Killed Walker's blind old lab. Motherfucker."

Karin kept quiet, gave Jonah a wink.

"How you feeling, sir?"

"Right as rain now, I think."

He had expected to be called son, but time had passed without him noticing and he realized that he was not much younger than Frank.

"I expect you had closer calls than this," said Frank.

"Yes. Many. I shouldn't be here."

"But you are. What's it like being back?"

Jonah thought carefully, searching for something new to impart to one whose taxes had sent him away for four years. "It's like the moment before a bubble bursts," he said, and watched the old man frown. As though the frown had been an act of speech, Jonah added, "I don't understand any of it either."

"Off you go then, Major Tom, and let our golden girl look after you. Sure wish I could get a deal like that."

They went back to the truck where Karin took her Magnum off the seat and put it in her shoulder bag. She slammed the doors and took his arm as they walked down the alley and across the road to her store. She said, "Frank will have that bear processed by midnight. I'll make you a necklace."

"Flying bear meat."

"Are you suffering that gravity sickness?"

"What's with the Major Tom thing?"

"That's what we call you. Major Tom."

She took him straight through to her quarters behind the store, straight into her bedroom and said, "Now, mister, off with those pants. I want my reward right now before I put you in the shower."

He had been with this type before. They were fun. He said, "So you want me all smelling of bear?"

She couldn't laugh since she was breathing too heavily and her eyes looked wild and intense as she pulled her own clothes off. He worked hard not to laugh. She got on top of him and went for her reward immediately. He held her hips tightly to keep her from flying off into oblivion.

* * *

He had never eaten bear loin before. It tasted dark and good and made him feel strong immediately. It reminded him of wild boar he had eaten in France. He did not tell Karin this. He didn't say anything about his life and, to her credit, after asking a couple personal questions and not getting answers, she talked of other things. There was always plenty to talk about. She usually came up to the cabin in the afternoons and cooked for him and they ate together after his work, and then went walking. She always had the Magnum with her, otherwise he would not have gone. He was ruined now for the outdoors. Just as always, death could come from anywhere. He had stopped running and had put on a bit of weight with all her cooking. After the walk she always wanted to have sex before going back down to the village. She was very attracted to him, wanted him all the time, and that stimulated him and kept him in the game, but usually he was glad when she left. He felt free when he could close the door behind her and read a novel. She never tried to stay the night in the cabin, but sometimes he stayed the night down at her place in back of the store. He realized that she was afraid. He was afraid of bears—and she was obviously afraid of the cabin at night.

He always slept heavily, but one night a noise woke him. It was a bear crying. Just a dream, but he turned all the lights on. Karin had made him a necklace of teeth in the manner of the region's natives, of which she was a quarter-blood. Old Frank was her uncle. Frank was curing the bear pelt because the cabin needed something on the floor. They all agreed it was too stark. Hell, it wasn't his place. He didn't wear the necklace unless she put it on him when they made love. For a long time he hated the bear and wanted it killed multiple times, wanted it tortured, but that suddenly went away when they brought him its teeth, and now he felt sorry for it and wished it had been smart enough to stick to scheduled sleeping times.

A few days later the rug arrived, brought by old Walker's grandsons, and with it ensued the full haunting of the cabin.

He had roughed out a first draft of the book, and indeed it had lots of bear about it but no bear displayed. He was pleased. He could work from this draft anytime, so it was okay to face the haunting and not pretend it wasn't happening. He knew it would happen eventually because he had brought it home from Space.

The head of the bear looked very dead and he avoided its eyes.

The first night the rug lay on the living room floor he was woken by crying. He went into the living room and the bearskin was rising up off the floor as if some asshole was underneath it, trying to frighten him. It stayed like that for a while and then rose into the pitch of the ceiling and waited there, hovering. This was not as frightening as being chased by a bear that wanted to tear you apart, but it was frightening enough, and he stood with tingling skin, watching something happen that he did not understand. His hair became electrified when the pelt suddenly flew down and made for the fireplace. There was no fire tonight and the logs banked up for the next fire prevented the pelt from stuffing itself up the chimney headfirst. He turned all the lights on and left the pelt where it was.

It was late, but he rang Karin.

He had never heard her so quiet. He knew he was going to start learning things, and wondered if there was really anything else he needed to know about how fucked up people are and how it only takes one to fuck up a family, and that magic and the supernatural weren't so strange. And he didn't really believe his own eyes. Even when he saw it, he didn't. It was always traceable back to people: disorganized, cruel, egocentric, ignorant, obsessed, immature… stupid. Like that damn old bear coming out of hibernation for some fool reason of its own.

He made himself a big mug of hot chocolate and sat by the fireplace, sipping and gazing at the pelt, which looked like a concentrated mass of bats, a billion black flies—a quid of black semen loaded into the devil's shotgun, ready to be fired into the world to spread discord—a black hole.

He'd wait for her—poor old Karin—who was older than she looked and even more haunted than he. She was on her way up with sandalwood and sage, but she would not do the ritual properly because she would not want to involve Uncle Frank as she should. Her attention would be torn between getting herself clear of all the crap that had gathered around her and getting herself permanent with the interesting stranger. She had no self-discipline, and for all her pride in her Native quarter she was as white as snow. She would want to do a little ritual and then nail the pelt to the floor. Nail down the bear, nail hard, and keep nailing him.

Oh well, the draft is done, Jonah thought. Let's see what happens next.

Shift

Nancy Holder

He is the lobster man.

He is so old, such a fixture of Greystone Bay, many of the young inhabitants don't know his name. To the littlest ones, it doesn't occur to them that he has one at all.

But Allen Hill, the lobster man, has lived a life.

Hard as it may be to believe, he walked the cobbles, worn even in his day, to Greystone Elementary School; worked a job in Mr. Lindquist's factory, married a local girl, and fathered a red-headed boy named James.

Hard for the young ones to believe.

Harder still for the lobster man to believe.

It seems he has lived this way forever:

One plate, one cracked china cup, a cupboard filled with tins of dog food. Doilies his wife knitted decaying on the worn arms of a single upholstered chair. A hot plate that works intermittently. A black-and white television, a thick woolen sweater covering dusty old-man's pants and cheap socks his daughter-in-law sends from California.

Four walls, two uncracked. A separate bathroom containing a tub with clawed feet. Curtains wafted by so many summer breezes they looked like the moldy remains of a winding-sheet. Linoleum that crumbles beneath his brown corduroy house slippers. A daybed. A lamp. An empty fishbowl.

About the dog food: he doesn't have a dog, though it is obvious to his son and daughter-in-law that he should have one ("Keep you company, Dad, you're alone too much"). The shelves in the cupboard bulge with dog food. And each night, he looks them over, deciding—

—chicken parts? hearts and livers?

—because there are nights for scraps and nights for organs— he knows this to be true, though he couldn't have explained just why to another living soul. There just are, and this, the choosing of the dog food, is one of the few uncertain factors in his existence—one plate, one cup, one chair, but dozens of tins of kidneys and livers and other bits and pieces of sacrificial cattle.

He selects the tin of food, then takes up a large hoop almost three feet in diameter draped with a net of fine wire mesh, this lobster man, and leaves his single room to walk the fog-laden streets of Greystone Bay.

He doesn't feel the cobbles beneath his feet anymore; doesn't hear the keening of the foghorns out at sea. He doesn't look in the windows of the shops and offices as he passes: the ghosts are all still there, as are the faces of the men and women among whom he has lived and aged all these years, the changeless years of Greystone Bay. He carries his dog food in the pocket of his baggy, dusty trousers, a dark blue cap hiding his eyes from the misted streetlights. His grey hair curls around the collar of his pea coat. He never cuts it; it never grows.

Each night the soles of his boots—his feet are cold in the Californian socks—each night they buff the same scores of cobbles on his way to Waterford Tavern. For decades he has walked along Woodbine Street, holding on to the hoop, feeling for the dog food— and it occurs to him once that he must have rubbed and buffed and lightly sanded the cobbles of his ever-unmodified path, perhaps just one-hundredth of an inch in his lifetime, but that he must have affected them. And yet, the cobbles look no different than when he was a boy—he had been a *boy,* once, that lobster man.

Nothing looks any different. Nothing in the entire grey town of Greystone Bay.

Except the faces of his friends. Lines etched like scrimshaw into ivory, where once-robust youth bloomed; lips as grey as Greystone fog; eyes rheumy, hands shaky. Old-man tremors, old-man talk. Old Man Death taking one now and again.

Allen Hill sighs heavily and walks along the quay, shifting the weight of the hoop. Then he pushes open the double doors of the Waterford Tavern and goes in.

His friends are there—there are four; he makes it five at the varnished circular table closest to the potbellied stove. Hiram, Wayne, Joe, Ken—bare, short names for men whose lives have been pared down by years and circumstance—one cup, one chair, the embarrassment of being taken in on holidays, or worse yet, being pitied because no one did take them in. Spare old men—whose lives have been long, perhaps overly so. With spare faces of scrimshaw ivory that don't exactly smile as Allen Hill walks in, but register his entrance and welcome him, in their way.

He sets down his hoop behind the door. Without being asked, Ruth, the daughter of the tavernkeeper and the only barmaid, brings a mug of ale and leaves it in front of one of three empty chairs at the table while Allen divests himself of his pea coat and cap. At the other two places, beer mugs turned upside down gleam in the tavern light.

The can of dog food thumps against the arm of the chair as he sits down and gestures his thanks at the woman. Once a girl, once an infant. He went to church for her christening. Now she looks like a young matron, as Anne was when she died.

"Evening," Wayne says for the four.

"What's new?" Allen replies, and they all chuckle grimly. Nothing ever is.

"Bagged a bufflehead today," Joe offers. "Big one."

The men nod. Then they drink their ale and sit in companionable silence. After so many years, words can be a nuisance. They have long ago told each other everything they ever planned to, and a few things they have not. The years of divulged secrets, blurted wishes, murmured regrets are their collective culture, the Old Men's Culture, set in stone like epitaphs. They are a society of five, though once there were seven of them, seven friends and old mates.

Each time one of them dies, they turn over his mug—there is a special rack over the bar for them, with seven hooks (though only five are used now, and those in the shape of a star)—and set it in front of his accustomed place at the table. Ruth washes them and sets them out each night before the survivors arrive. Tom Blouseter, the resident artist of Greystone Bay, painted the scene four years ago when they turned George Tooney's over after his funeral.

When touched with melancholy, Allen stares at the two empty, upside-down mugs and wonders, *When*?

On bad nights, he hopes, *Tonight*?

He drinks his ale slowly, for these days he takes only one because it makes him sleepy and he might have a long night to face. Across the room, a young man punches a song selection on the jukebox, something jumpy with a refrain that goes "all night long." The man raps a drumroll on the face of the jukebox, then dances back to his place at the bar.

"Kids today." Hiram gestures at Ruth, who comes for his empty mug and spirits it away.

Kids today. *Greystone Bay sucks, Dad.* That was how James said it. *You suck.*

No, he didn't voice that last part.

But he had meant it, his red-headed child who looked so much like Anne that it used to make Allen weep. James hated the grey town with its grey fog, hated his grey father for living there and for being grey. He hitchhiked to California as soon as he graduated from high school. There were some bad years, and then the boy straightened himself out. Now he works for a bank and has a wife.

—who sends Allen socks that make his toes ache with cold; but they are, in an indirect way, gifts from James, and so the lobster man wears them—

—who doesn't understand why a man with no dog has so much dog food, even after he explained it to her when they came—once, just once—to visit.

"I'd better shove off now," Allen says to the others. "I've got to get to work."

They all nod. No one says goodbye. They simply watch him drain his mug and push away from the table.

All night long, all night

Allen walks from the tavern and turns another corner. Now he is directly in front of the Atlantic View Hotel. Forty yards beyond, the pier stretches into the black marble water, its end dissolved in fog.

He hefts the hoop and feels for the dog food. There is a glow in the fog that tells him the moon is full, though he can't see it. The diffuse light rings the streetlamps and drizzles in pools of damp at their bases.

Four years ago, a young Jewish man from Manhattan visited Greystone Bay—jogging all the way down the seaboard, no doubt, attaché case in hand—and declared it the perfect site to develop into another Nantucket. He nearly swooned when he saw the cobbled streets; and the Atlantic View, where he stayed, threw him into a fit of ecstasy. He clasped his hands at the sight of the four old sailing ships bobbing in the water.

"Quaint, untouched, unspoiled!" he chanted as he viewed the old brick buildings. "Perfect! Look at that quay—I see shops! Boutiques! Those clapboards! I see condos on North Hill—I mean, *luxe* housing," he assured the Chamber of Commerce, who stared at him blankly. "I could make this town for you!"

Much discussion followed. There was talk of a referendum. Allen and his friends said little, except to shake their heads. And just when it looked as if Greystone Bay might have its quaintness restored by a quay filled with boutiques and a hill crammed with condominiums, the young Jewish man returned.

And saw the fog.

It rolled in that night like bolts of grey flannel, like silver cotton wool blanketing housetops and treetops and the illuminated sign of the hotel, rendering everything invisible. It swirled around Allen Hill's ankles as he walked from the tavern to the pier. In all his years he had never seen it so bad.

The Jewish young man lost all interest in making Greystone Bay. He couldn't see shoppers groping through the murk, cars grinding into each other like lost ships. He left for Manhattan and was never heard from again. Life went back to its original form, its unvarying texture, except for the death, seven months later, of George Tooney. Old age, the doctor said. A lifetime of bad habits.

The fog was light the day of his funeral. Afterward, Allen himself turned George's mug over at the Waterford Tavern.

His toes are stinging by the time he reaches the wooden box in the middle of the pier. His fingers have etched a groove in the lid and they fit into it automatically as he opens it. Inside lie a battered picnic cooler, a pair of gloves, a package of rubber bands, and a sandwich wrapped in cellophane.

He pulls the cooler out first, then picks up the sandwich and sets it on the pier. He isn't hungry yet; he might be there some hours and need it later.

About the sandwich: the youngest Peixe boy makes one up for him every night and leaves it with the emptied cooler. Lobster salad for the lobster man. "Best of the catch," Juliao assures him. "For you, always the best."

Which is, of course, only fair.

For here he stands in the cold, grey night, a few feet above the black water that lap-slaps at the pylons that will never support Greystone Fashions and Greystone Creperie. He stands all alone, impassive, a granite man, while others sleep and drink and savor each other. But for him, solitude, a night swimming in fog, a hoop, a tin of kidneys,

a lobster salad sandwich.

A son who comes but once to see him, a daughter-in-law who doesn't want children because she is afraid of stretch marks. Two dead friends, four living ones, oh, please, four...

It is a calm night. A typical night. What's new? There, on the pier, absolutely nothing.

He fills the cooler with bay water by carrying it off the pier to the shore and dipping it into the bay. After he carries it back, careful not to slosh it on such a chilly night, he pulls his key chain out of his pocket—one key only, for his front door, and a can opener—and sets about indenting the can lid with six triangular-shaped openings. Enough to let a little dog food out, but not enough to let anything devour it.

He attaches the tin to three wire spokes that point toward the center of the hoop. He sticks the wires through three of the triangular openings and bends them backward. He makes the projections out of clothes hangers, which Hiram gives him every once in a while: Hiram used to own a dry-cleaning business.

The odor of dog food is on his fingers; he wipes them absently on his pants before he puts on his thick leather gloves. He lowers the hoop into the thick waters of the bay with a length of chain. A passerby (who is not a native of the Bay, and therefore would not know of the lobster man) would think he is fishing.

Down, down, until it rests on the bottom. After all this time, he knows exactly how far to lower it. Then he glances up at the whitest part of the fog—where the moon floats in the sky—and waits.

It usually takes about fifteen minutes. Sure enough, there is a tug-tug-tug, ever so subtle, that a less experienced person wouldn't notice.

But Allen Hill is the lobster man. Quickly he pulls in the chain and raises the hoop from the water.

Inside thrashes a lobster. Allen nods at it. With the unconscious ease of decades, be lowers the net to the pier without letting the creature out; grabs it, secures its tail against its body with a rubber band, and dumps it into the cooler.

Lobster salad.

He lowers the hoop and the tin of dog food back into the water. And waits.

It takes twenty-five minutes this time. Well within range of his experience. After he drops the second lobster into the cooler, he eats his sandwich. He steps·on the toes of his shoes to wake up his chilled feet, then lowers the hoop one more time.

Five lobsters are his quota. He doesn't remember how he and the Peixe brothers, who own the town fish market, decided on five, but five it is. How ironic. There are five old men now. Maybe if it were seven…

When? Tonight?

Three, four, five come in quick succession. Lobsters to the slaughter. The Peixe brothers suggested he leave the filled cooler in the box, which they retrieve the following morning, and he is always grateful he doesn't have to lug the heavy object home.

He unfastens the tin of dog food and plops it into the cooler—last supper—and gathers up his hoop.

Then he trudges home as he always does.

Always.

The lobster man.

* * *

The next night, he walks to the tavern, hefting his hoop. He lays it by the door; Ruth appears with his ale. His friends sit in their accustomed places; the empty mugs, too.

"What's new?" Allen asks.

"This duck," Joe says. He shakes his head a little before he sips his ale. "I tell you, there was something about it."

Allen looks at the others.

"He's talking about a duck," Hiram explains.

Joe goes duck hunting. One duck for Mendel the butcher, that is his quota.

"And there's something… different about the drake I caught." Joe pulls a pipe and a pouch of tobacco from his jacket.

They sit without speaking. After an interval, Hiram frowns, pulling his mouth down so slightly that a passerby wouldn't notice it.

"Joe, I looked at it. It was just a plain old duck."

Joe scoops out the wad of old tobacco and plops it into an ashtray, then knocks his pipe sharply on the side of the table.

"You're not a duck hunter. You don't see the things I do."

"I've hunted ducks, Joe."

"Not like I have. Not nearly every day, like me."

Allen is startled by the conversation. These are too many words for the Old Men's Culture, sliding beneath an undercurrent of tension—not much, but the ripples are obvious. The five never quarrel anymore; they are too old and they have settled all there is to settle among them.

"Well, then, tell us what was different about it," Hiram says.

Joe glances at Allen as if for assistance. The lobster man returns his look blankly—he knows less about it than the others, having come in last—then shrugs and picks up his ale.

Joe sighs. "I told you, I can't explain it. But I know that duck is… isn't… I threw it out. I didn't eat it."

"So it was diseased, then," Allen ventures.

"No." Joe wads the new tobacco into the bowl of his pipe without looking at the others. Yet his fingers betray his frustration as he tamps the tobacco. "I mean, I don't know if it was or not. I just knew I…"

He flushes. "I didn't want to touch it anymore."

Again he looks at Allen, who lowers his eyes to his mug. He wonders if his friend is getting senile. He wonders if that is what's behind the too-cheerful calls from California ("Weather's great out here, Dad! Why don't you come for a visit?"). Have James and his wife decided he is getting stupid in the head? He muses about the despair that washes over him at night

all night long, all night

and makes him stare at the empty beer mugs.

"There was something *wrong* with the damned duck," Joe mutters, and that is the end of the conversation.

About fifteen minutes later, Allen rises and leaves the tavern. No one has spoken another word.

* * *

The next day, Hiram comes knocking at Allen's door. (If at all possible, the old men never phone each other; they prefer to conduct their business in person. It is as if they do not trust the machinery, or do not believe the wires could pierce the fog sufficiently to carry their straining old voices to each other's houses.)

Allen has been in the pantry, contemplating his stock of dog food: he is fine; he won't need to call the market for some time. He seems to favor kidneys lately, though hearts take a close second.

"It's Joe," Hiram tells him. "He wants us all to go over to his place."

"Is he sick?" The image of Joe's beer mug flashes through Allen's mind. Down it goes, down and over

down and out

and Blouseter the artist paints another scene.

Hiram shrugs in response. Allen slides on his pea coat and cap and follows Hiram out the door.

Greystone Bay is a small town. Hiram and Allen both have walked the route to Joe's a million times, a hundred million. They walk without speaking, twisting and turning, and Allen thinks once to comment on the thinness of the fog for this time of year; but he never gets around to it.

Wayne and Ken are already at Joe's. It is Wayne who answers the door, face impassive save for one bushy white raised eyebrow.

"We're out back," he says, leading the two men through the cottage

one plate, one cracked china cup

and into the yard (one broken manual lawn mower, a thousand weeds, trees, a rotting teddy bear, a discarded gun rack).

Joe is crouched with his back to the men. He turns around and glances at the four, his gaze pausing at Allen. Then he gestures to something on the ground.

Allen and the others gather around him. Spread on a flattened plastic trash bag shimmer the remains of a small brown duck. Beside its severed but otherwise undamaged head lies a bloody hunting knife.

There is a long moment of studying the splayed carcass. Beady eyes, bleeding entrails. Allen bends down, winces at the arthritis in his knees, and straightens again.

Finally Joe lowers his head. "Can't you *see?*" His voice is low.

"No." Hiram nudges a wing.

"Don't touch it!" Joe cries.

Silence.

"What's wrong with it?" Allen asks. "Tell us."

Again a long look in his direction. "You're a hunter," Joe says. "You understand, don't you?"

A hunter. Allen has never thought of himself that way. He is the lobster man.

"There's nothing wrong with that duck." Hiram rises. "Not a thing."

After a while, they all go back inside. Joe halfheartedly offers everyone a beer which each man declines. They do their drinking at the Waterford Tavern.

Always have.

* * *

Allen is on the pier, waiting for the first lobster of the evening. He can see the lights in the windows of the Atlantic View, almost make out dim shapes in them

Listen, it is spring fogless night

and wishes himself inside the Waterford Tavern, drinking more ale with his friends. Joe is looking unwell these days; he says nothing more about his ducks, and the matter has dropped, but he is clearly troubled about something. Allen supposes that it is the ducks, but he doesn't ask. It is not part of the Old Men's Culture to pry.

("What's all this dog food for, Allen?" James's wife asked in a high, shocked voice. Her tone took Allen aback until later, after they had returned to California, he realized she thought he was eating it himself.)

He stands on the pier—why has he never gotten himself a chair? More to worry about, more baggage—and looks up at the moon, pale and thin behind streaks of grey.

Spring, fogless.

He is waiting for the first lobster, and as he lowers his gaze from the moon to the water he experiences a sense of disquiet.

He cocks his head. He can't understand the feeling, nor pinpoint its source. After a while, it fades, and he frowns when he realizes how much time has passed without a catch.

He smiles as much as the lobster man ever smiles with his grey face. That is the source of his unease—that no lobster has yet crept into his trap. They are slow tonight, his lobster salads, but then, there have been other slow nights.

The water is so calm. Still. He doesn't hear it lapping the pylons. But then, he hasn't heard, nor seen, nor smelled anything of Greystone Bay in years, that lobster man.

But it seems calmer than usual, that black marble sea.

There is a tugging. Allen grunts to himself and hoists the lobster net out of the water.

A good, fat one. He readies a rubber band around his fingers and prepares to grab the spiny creature.

He catches it as if by the scruff of the neck, avoiding the claws and the wildly thrashing tail. He bands the tail against the body with the movements of a calf roper.

Then, just as he is about to put it into the cooler, he stops. It doesn't smell right. No, that isn't it. Doesn't look right. No. It doesn't...

It doesn't.

Without knowing why, he unbands it and throws the lobster back.

Spring and fogless, all night long. It is the first night Allen can remember that he doesn't fill his quota. After he throws back the first one, no more appear. He waits for hours, until his toes can stand it no more, and goes home.

* * *

The next night, he finds a lobster salad sandwich in his cooler, as always, with a note from Juliao: *Good* Sorte *tonight!*

But he has bad luck that night, too. Empty-handed once more, he pockets the sandwich and takes it home with him, but forgets to put it in his refrigerator and has to throw it away in the morning.

By this time, Joe has begun to watch Allen when he comes into the tavern. He says nothing, but Allen notes a flicker in the man's eyes when Hiram asks, "Feeling okay?" and Allen nods.

"Okay as an old man can feel," he responds, which makes the others nod (slightly, so that a passerby wouldn't notice).

They say little else. Allen drinks his beer. Then he leaves the tavern.

He wonders if a disease has killed off all the lobsters. Nothing like this has ever happened before. His cooler is still empty. He stands one, two, three hours

tug, tug, tug

and finally raises the net, rubber band at the ready

and he *knows* what Joe was talking about.

Something not quite right. But what? He stares at the lobster he has just dumped into the cooler. A thin chill skitters up his spine. What? He can't see anything different. He can only feel it.

He keeps looking at the lobster while he waits for the next one. His stomach is heavy, as if from eating too much, and after a while he pulls up the net—empty, save for the can of beef hearts. He dumps most of the water from the cooler, mindful not to touch the lobster, and drapes the net over his wooden box. One night won't ruin it, and he can't carry both it and the cooler.

He takes the lobster home. He sets it on the floor and sits on his bed, and stares at it. It is an ordinary looking lobster about a foot long, with two large (but not unusually large) claws, antennae, and a stiff tail fan.

After a while, he shakes his head. ("Weather's great out here, Dad! Why not come for a visit?" There will never be any grandchildren, ever, because James's wife doesn't want to ruin her figure. He has a vision of himself, mired in senility, feeding dog food to a screaming toddler.)

There is nothing wrong with the damned thing. He knows that now. Feeling foolish, he changes into a pair of heavy flannel pajamas, brushes his teeth, and climbs into bed.

But sleep does not come easily that night to the lobster man. He guesses it is because he was in bed too early, but his consciousness is focused on the cooler, dimly outlined in the dark room. This lobster, this

thing.

He turns on the light and peers into the cooler. Not a damned thing wrong. Maybe tomorrow he will cut it open and make lobster salad with it. He hopes the Peixe brothers aren't getting impatient with him.

Later, in the night, his peripheral awareness tells him of sloshing in the cooler, perhaps of scuttling... he thinks of his dog food, a pantry of it. He thinks of spiny legs, crawling beneath the blanket, creeping past his ankle, his calf, his sore, cold knees...

He wakes up and makes himself some chamomile tea, which he drinks from his cracked china cup.

About the chamomile tea: he doesn't remember buying it. He doesn't remember how often he drinks it.

He doesn't remember how old he is.

That lobster man.

* * *

The grey daylight shines on the shell of the lobster as Allen stares at the creature. Nothing wrong with it at all. He has been foolish. He decides he will take it to the Peixe brothers as a peace offering and catch twice as many lobsters that night, even if he has to stand there until dawn.

He dresses and eats, then hefts the cooler in his arms and starts toward the fish market. The air is brisk, the gulls wheeling above him in the fog. He can't see them, and he imagines himself inside a fishbowl, swimming through the fog; and above the mists, the clear surface of the world where the gulls and other creatures live.

Other creatures.

He turns this way and that, swimming through his fog, and then he stumbles on a cobble.

Stumbles, he who has worn those cobbles down—and drops the cooler. The lobster flies out and rolls into the street, disappearing beneath the tires of the Peixe brothers' truck as it turns the comer.

An image flashes through Allen's mind, accompanied by relief: *Now he will see inside it.*

But he can't, because there's really nothing left.

* * *

In the tavern: a bad night, because he thinks they all are glancing at him, wondering about him. Joe looks pasty, almost angry, but he says nothing. He is working on his third mug of ale when Allen wordlessly leaves.

On the pier: a bad night.

Another lobster, and this one as… unsettling as the other. He knows how Joe felt, the frustration, the confusion—

And wonders if it is part of the Old Men's Culture, as he had wonders before about his despair *(tonight?)*.

This time Allen sits on the pier, legs dangling over the side as when he was a boy—a *boy,* that lobster man—and looks at the lobster floating like a dead thing in the cooler.

The bay is too calm, the night too clear. For a moment he thinks he's in another town.

But there is the Atlantic View; there the never-to-be quaint quay of the never-to-be-made town, the fogbound town of Greystone Bay, uneasily free of fog.

It is spring, fogless.

But no, even in summer there is fog; always, always some few wisps of grey cotton wool.

Always.

Why he takes the lobster back to his room he has no idea. And why he sits there in the night, peering at it. And why he is still up beside it in the sunlight. He doesn't move all day, keeping a vigil, as it were, with the thing that seems smarmy, not right, unnatural

thing

not diseased, not… *bad*

is it?

He crosses his arms as he scrutinizes it, hunched, his arthritic knees hurting as the room grows chilly. He balls his fists. He doesn't want to touch it. At the thought, he shudders, then goes to brush his teeth.

He sits all day beside the lobster. A few times, he reaches out his hand, then recoils.

He must have dozed; when he stirs, it is dark in the room
scuttle, scuttle-scuttle, no, he hears nothing in the blackness
and the hairs on the back of his neck stand on end
when he reaches to turn on the light. Suppose the lobster has escaped?

Senile. He grits his teeth and flicks the switch. He takes a breath before he turns around to face the cooler. And the thing inside it.

* * *

A bad night: how on earth can he be lost? He knows Greystone Bay better than he knows his own son, his James. He knows each inch of each cobble, each building. He knows the shapes and forms within the fog—so thick tonight, but that doesn't matter. He can find his way blindfolded.

Yet the streets all look the same, as if they have melted into each other. One amorphous mass of grey paste, grey wax, melting and running—floating, really—and he, the maze-maker, stumbling inside it. How can he be lost?

He only wants to find the tavern, with its lights and its potbellied stove, tables of varnished wood
upside-down mugs
and his friends, who at that very moment must be sitting silently, drinking ale, perhaps wondering why he is so late.

For time moves inside the floating paste; he knows that, though he doesn't know the contents of the windows he passes, nor the texture of the cobbles beneath his feet. Time moves, and he is lost, and he can't understand it.

That lobster... and tonight he will try again, though he is beginning to lose hope. Tonight he will apologize to Joe, in his spare-old-man's way, perhaps with a mumbled word, a glance, a shrug. An implicit gesture, unrecognizable to a passerby, but understood within the society of the Old Men's Culture. He will apologize for not understanding about the ducks.

If he ever finds Joe.

For is he not moving in slow motion? Are the streets whirling past, breaking up, rising into the fog to surface in the clear world of the gulls? He flails for a lamppost to catch his balance; but it is gone, missing from the spot where it has stood for decades, for as long as Allen himself has stood.

Where are the buildings he knows so well? Where are the Peixe brothers' fish market and Mendel's shop with the sausages in the windows?

(Where he used to hang his exotic prizes, the ducks Joe shot for him, and which have been missing for weeks.)

Where is it all?

"Weather's great, Dad. Why don't you come for a visit?"

He labors on in the grey paste of Greystone Bay, searching. He thinks of the lobster, still floating in the cooler, and wraps his coat more closely around himself. His toes burn with cold.

Listen, it is spring

and then he rounds a corner and sees the neon sign of the tavern.

He nearly weeps with relief. With both hands he opens the door and steps into the room.

The grey paste swirls around him. Everything is different. The walls are a different color; the bar, no longer made of wood; the jukebox, no longer a leftover fifties consolidation of chrome and red plastic but sleek, streamlined, silver.

And Ruth, who stands at the different bar *en profil:* old.

Older than Allen Hill himself.

He gasps audibly, falling against the door. At that moment Ruth turns, sees him, and screams. He has never seen such a look of terror on anyone's face before.

Everyone in the tavern screams. They jump out of their chairs and back away, huddling together around the jukebox.

"What?" Allen cries, looking behind himself. He hurries toward the group. "What?"

His gaze leaps to his old table.

No one sits at it. In front of seven empty places, seven mugs rest upside down.

Seven...

"What? What?" Allen pleads, holding out his grey arms, his arms that once were pink and muscled from working in Mr. Lindquist's factory; that once held his wife and cradled his son; that lifted thousands of lobsters from the Greystone Bay.

That finally touched the one in the cooler...

And then he remembers: he searched the pantry

before he left. The dog food was all gone.

The lobster was gone.

It is spring, fogless...

All gone, all gone.

"What?" he screams.

Ruth's father, the tavernkeeper—unbelievably ancient—raises a rifle from beneath the bar.

"Jesus, god, Jesus, god," the man whispers as he takes aim.

Allen begins to cry. As the man pulls the trigger, Allen flings open his arms.

"Why?" he shrieks in a thin, high voice.

Old Man Death coming for one now and again—

shift

He is the lobster man.

About the Authors

Roger Barr

Roger Barr is the author of a novel, *The Treasure Hunt*, the short story collection *Getting Ready for Christmas & Other Stories* and seven works of non-fiction, including biographies of Richard Nixon and Malcolm X written for young adults. A past Minnesota State Arts Board Grant recipient, he was the winner of The Loft's 2013 Spring Writing Contest, after receiving honorable mention in 2012. His play *Decoration Day* was a winner of the Lakeshore Players' Ten Minute Play Festival contest and was produced in 2010.

Karen Bovenmyer

Karen Bovenmyer earned an MFA in Creative Writing: Popular Fiction from the University of Southern Maine. She teaches and mentors students at Iowa State University and serves as the Nonfiction Assistant Editor of *Escape Artists' Mothership Zeta Magazine*. Her short stories and poems appear in more than 20 publications and her first novel will be available Spring 2017. http://karenbovenmyer.com/

David Culberson

David Culberson grew up in small town middle America. After a higher education in a warmer climate, he spent much of the next three decades living and mixing with the cultures of the Caribbean, Mexico and Lake Superior, where he pioneered sustainable development and built several low-impact resort properties. He is also the author of the novels *Back Time on Love City: The Carnival Never Stopped*, and *Alterio's Motive*.

Terry Faust

Terry Faust's enjoyment of speculative fiction writing developed from a love of drawing, photographing, and making films of unusual subjects. He is a still photographer and video producer. The whimsical humor and biting satire of speculative fiction authors Kurt Vonnegut, Terry Bisson, Tom Holt, Glen Cook and Terry Pratchett have inspired him as has some urban fantasy, including that by Emma Bull. His young adult urban fantasy, *Bearer of the Pearls*, will be released by North Star Press in 2017. He has been an assistant organizer of the Minnesota Speculative Fiction Writers Network since 2005.

Nancy Holder

Nancy Holder is a New York Times bestselling author of over 80 novels and 200 short stories. She has received 5 Bram Stoker awards from the Horror Writers Association and a Young Adult Pioneer Award from RT Booksellers. Her short fiction has appeared in many "Best Of" anthologies. She is known for writing material for *Buffy the Vampire Slayer*, *Hellboy*, Sherlock Holmes, Nancy Drew, and other "universes," and she wrote the novelizations of *Crimson Peak* and the new *Ghostbusters*. Her latest novel is the young adult thriller *The Rules*. Socialize @nancyholder and visit her at www.nancyholder.com.

CM Kerley

CM Kerley grew up in a small town cut off from the world by sugar cane that would whisper on warm windy days. From her bedroom window she could see an abandoned menacing old sugar mill near the forest. Every night she saw strange flashing lights and heard unnatural noises coming from the mill – obviously ghosts and sorcerers at war. She bought her first comic book at age 9, got her first adult library card at 11, and at 15 completed her first fantasy novel. She still sees lights and hears noises – thinks they might be cars or airplanes – but believes magic makes a better story.

Carolyn Killion

A bit of a dreamer but a do'er. Head is in the clouds, but feet firmly on the ground. A list maker, cookie baker, perpetual student of string theory, bumbling hiker, cavorting canoeist, fantastical writer, erstwhile fisher, winter sun midday napper, thirsty seeker of knowledge, eager traveler. Lives in Grantsburg, WI.

Cynthia Kraack

Cynthia Kraack is an author of fiction and short stories. *The High Cost of Flowers* won two 2014 Midwest Book Awards, taking first in both Literary Fiction and Contemporary Fiction. Her debut work, *Minnesota Cold*, won the 2009 Northeastern Minnesota Book Award for Fiction. She also wrote the *Ashwood* trilogy, a speculative fiction family saga. *Glimmer Train*, *Big Muddy Literary Journal* and the Hal Prize competition have recognized her short stories. Her MFA comes from the University of Southern Maine's Stonecoast Program in Creative Writing. She is a founding board member of Write On, Door County.

Ian Graham Leask

Ian Graham Leask was born and raised in the London area. He is lucky to have had an unhappy childhood. He started writing at fifteen and has never stopped. After a year in Germany, where he worked as a meat porter and wrote poetry, he settled in Minneapolis, graduated from the University of Minnesota with degrees in English and writing. He is a teacher, literary consultant, publisher, and is the author of *The House of Large Sizes*, *The Wounded* and other stories about sons and fathers. He co-hosts KFAI's literary radio show *Write On! Radio* and lives in Minneapolis with frequent spells in London.

Steve McEllistrem

Steve McEllistrem has been a writer and editor for more than 20 years and is currently the science fiction and fantasy editor for

Calumet Editions. He also produces and hosts *Write On! Radio* on KFAI in the Twin Cities, where he interviews local, national and international authors. In addition to many works of non-fiction, he is the author of the Susquehanna Virus series: *The Devereaux Dilemma*, *The Devereaux Disaster*, *The Devereaux Decision* – which was a finalist for a Minnesota Book Award, a Midwest Book Award and an International Book Award – and *The Devereaux Deity*, released in 2016, and a finalist for both an International Book Award and a Midwest Book Award.

Lyda Morehouse

By day, Lyda Morehouse is a mild-mannered, award-winning science fiction writer; at night, she transforms into best-selling paranormal author Tate Hallaway. Between her two personas, Lyda has published 14 novels via various imprints of Penguin Random House. Most notably, she has won the Special Citation of Excellence Philip K. Dick Award for *Apocalypse Array* and the Shamus Award for *Archangel Protocol*. You can easily find both Lyda and Tate on most social media sites or at www. lydamorehouse.com. She lives in St. Paul, Minnesota.

Charley B. Murphy

C. B. Murphy is a writer, graphic novelist and painter. In his professional career, Murphy has worked in mining, industrial metals, and traveled globally designing and selling consumer products. Murphy has written several graphic novels including *The Second Mongolian Invasion* and *Nuclear Pup*. His pop surrealist paintings continue to be widely exhibited. He is the author of a young adult novel *Cute Eats Cute* (Calumet Editions) and the novel *End of Men* (Zoographico Press). He is currently working on a novel with his son entitled *Bardo Zsa Zsa* and a sequel to *Cute Eats Cute* entitled *Cute Gets Ugly*.

Bill Nemmers

Bill Nemmers was born in Iowa. After college and two years with the US Army in Europe, he worked as an Architect in Boston. He then opened his own Architecture and Planning office in Maine for three decades and now lives in St. Paul, Minnesota. He has published a novel, *CRUDE*, set in North Dakota, is about to publish a novel which investigates certain strange occurrences during the Great Cold War, and is working on a non-fiction book about Prince Henry 'The Navigator' of Portugal and his influence on 15th century Cosmology and Architecture.

Rick Polad

Rick Polad teaches Earth Science, plays jazz trumpet, and volunteers with the Coast Guard on Lake Michigan. Rick edited the English version of *Living With Nuclei*, the memoirs of Japanese physicist, Motoharu Kimura, and is a managing editor with his publisher, Calumet Editions. Rick has published four Spencer Manning mysteries and is working on the fifth.

Pedro Ponce

Pedro Ponce is the author of *Stories After Goya* (Tree Light Books) and the novel *Dreamland*, forthcoming from Satellite Press. His short fiction has appeared in *Ploughshares*, *Gigantic*, *PANK*, *Copper Nickel*, and other journals. His stories have also been featured in the anthologies *Sudden Fiction Latino* (edited by Robert Shapard, James Thomas, and Ray Gonzalez) and *The Beacon Best of 2001* (edited by Junot Díaz). A 2012 National Endowment for the Arts fellow in creative writing, he teaches fiction and literary theory at St. Lawrence University.

G. Bernhard Smith

G. Bernhard Smith writes both speculative and literary fiction. His stories have been short listed for the *Chicago Tribune*'s Nelson Algren Short Story Award, The American Fiction Short Story Award and The Faulkner-Wisdom Literary Prize, among others. He earned his undergraduate degree in Computer Science from the University of New Orleans, and his Master of Fine Arts in Creative Writing from Hamline University in St. Paul. A native of New Orleans, he now lives in Burnsville, Minnesota, with his wife Jill.